ENTANGLED

HARLEIGH BECK

This is a work of fiction. Names, characters, organizations, places, events and incidents are either products of the author's imagination or are used fictitiously.

Copyright © 2022 by Harleigh Beck

All rights reserved.

No part of this book may be reproduced in any form or by any electronic or mechanical means, including information storage and retrieval systems, without written permission from the author, except for the use of brief quotations in a book review.

Cover design: 3Crows Author Services

Editing: Chris Williams

Proofreading: Green Proofreads

*Not suitable for readers under 18

For the lovers of dirty-talking fictional men who slap your kitty and demand that you call them 'Daddy.' This one is for you.

TRIGGER WARNING

Entangled is a dark erotic, suspense novella. This book isn't a romance and doesn't guarantee a happy ending. It's very dark and contains disturbing scenes that may be triggering for some readers. This includes sexually explicit content, degradation, breath play, voyeurism, death of a loved one, a taboo age-gap relationship, murder, dubious cheating, and threats of violence.

PROLOGUE
WILLOW, AGE 10

"SHOULD THEY KISS?" I ask my best friend, Chloe, as I brush my barbie's hair while she roots through the box filled with clothes and dolls that we brought out to her front yard. The warm sun heats my freckled shoulders. Her dad, Mr. Reid, mowed the lawn this morning, so now it smells of freshly cut grass that sticks to my knees. Chloe holds up a tuxedo and proceeds to change her Ken doll's clothes. "I think they should get married. Look in the box for a wedding dress."

I've always coveted Chloe's extensive Barbie collection. Mr. Reid spoils her. My mom doesn't want to buy me nice things.

I change my Barbie's clothes, and we hold them up next to each other. Chloe's mischievous eyes find mine as she says in her deepest voice, "I now pronounce you husband and wife." We smash Barbie and Ken's mouths together while making kissy noises.

Chloe breaks into giggles first, and I soon follow.

"Look what I got for my birthday," Dylan calls out to us from the sidewalk, where he stands with a skateboard in his hands. Chloe is up on her feet first. She has always liked

Dylan. I don't; he's annoying with his big smile and blue eyes. My Barbie and Chloe's Ken lie abandoned on the grass when I join them.

"My dad got it for me for my eleventh birthday," Dylan boasts.

"I don't know how you dare use it. I would break a leg."

"It's easy. Want me to teach you?"

Chloe's high pigtails sway as she quickly shakes her head. I step forward. "I'd like to try."

"Okay, yeah, sure." Dylan places it down on the ground, and I tentatively put my foot on it. It feels unstable.

"Keep your toes pointed forward and push off with the other foot, then do this." Dylan demonstrates how to step on.

How difficult can it be? I follow his instructions, but it's a lot harder than I anticipated. I quickly lose my balance and fall to the ground as I roll down the street.

"Oh, shit." Dylan runs up to me and crouches down. "Are you okay?"

My knee is bleeding, and the sting has me wincing. Dylan goes to help me up, but Mr. Reid cuts across the grass with Chloe close on his heels. "What happened?"

"Willow fell off the skateboard."

Mr. Reid crouches down in front of me and inspects my wound with gentle fingers. I've always been jealous of Chloe for having a dad who cares. I've never met mine. I don't even know who he is.

"Let's get you cleaned up inside." He helps me to my feet, and Chloe smiles at me as I hobble past her. She doesn't follow. Not now that Dylan is here and ready to show her his tricks.

When I join Mr. Reid in the kitchen, he grabs me by my hips and lifts me up on the counter. My feet dangle in the air while I watch him dig in the cupboard for band-aids.

"You should have worn kneepads."

"I didn't know."

"It's okay," he says, gently lifting my leg beneath my knee and resting my sandalled foot on his stomach. He cleans the wound and applies a pink band-aid with white unicorns. I stare at him the entire time, wondering if this is what it's like to have a dad. Or a parent who cares. My mom never cleans my wounds. She tells me to go away, to make less noise.

"There, good as new." Mr. Reid helps me down. "Be careful out there."

"Thank you."

I join Chloe and Dylan outside in the warm afternoon sun. Dylan rides down the street and then back. "Check this out." He does a flip, and Chloe claps her hands together excitedly.

"That was so cool!"

Dylan beams, kicking the board up into his hand. "Yeah?"

My eyes roll while Chloe nods eagerly. She's become obsessed with boys this summer, especially Dylan. He goes to the same school as us and is a year older. I don't understand what's so interesting about boys. They're annoying, always interrupting us when Barbie is about to get her happily ever after with Ken. And they steal your best friend. I especially don't understand what is so fascinating about Dylan. He's the most annoying boy of all. He's tall for his age, his hair is a constant mess, and he always has streaks of mud somewhere. If not on his cheek, then on his tanned arms.

I sit back down on the grass and pick up my Barbie. The wedding dress is stupid, so I tear it off her and select another one while Chloe continues gushing over Dylan and his stupid skateboard.

As I shift, my eyes catch on the unicorn band-aid on my knee. There's a red patch of blood on it.

The sound of a car draws my attention.

Mrs. Reid's Volvo parks in the driveway.

"Mom," Chloe calls out, waving as Mrs. Reid steps out and shoulders her bag. She's beautiful, with her hazel brown hair tied back and her knee-length skirt. Chloe's mom is always immaculately dressed and smiling. Unlike my mom, who rarely smiles and is always in a bad mood. Even at ten, I know Chloe and I are from different worlds.

Mr. Reid steps out of the house, embracing his wife. In that moment, I'm jealous of Chloe and her perfect life. My Barbie will never get her Ken and the Dreamhouse.

CHAPTER 1
WILLOW
OCTOBER 27TH, 2015

7 YEARS LATER

"MOM?" I call out, emerging from my bedroom. The house is quiet except for the grandfather clock in the hallway. My heart sinks, which is stupid. Even after all this time, I wish she would be here to say good morning. To give a damn about her daughter. But she doesn't. Some things never change.

I eat breakfast alone in the kitchen. The radio is on to help me feel less empty inside. The silence is the worst. It's loud, and if I let it sneak in, it soon starts to scream.

I'm taking the last bite of my sandwich when the doorbell rings.

As Chloe enters, my face spreads in a smile.

"Where's my favorite bitch?"

Sliding my chair back, I join her in the hallway. She eyes my Chucks with distaste as I put them on.

"What?" I laugh.

"We need to get you a new wardrobe."

"What's wrong with my clothes this time?"

Chloe is very girly, and I'm not. She likes colors and heels while I prefer to dress in denim skirts and T-shirts. Sometimes I wear something colorful if I'm adventurous, but I don't venture away from my Chucks. Heels are off the table. I'd break my ankle.

"What does the quote say on your T-shirt today?"

I look down. "'The answer is no.'"

With an eye roll and a soft laugh, she walks out. I lock up, dropping the key in my bag. We're neighbors. I live next door, and Dylan's house is across the street from us.

When we're buckled up in her car, she lowers the roof and attempts a smile.

"How are you holding up?" I ask.

Today is the five-year anniversary of when her mother disappeared without a trace. She went to work one day and never came home. Chloe was never the same again. Beneath her convincing smile is the ghost of the girl I once knew.

Drawing in a deep sigh, she reverses out of the driveway. It's not until we're on the main road that she replies in a choked voice, "It would be so much easier if they had found a body, you know?"

"That way, you could have closure."

She nods, wringing the steering wheel. "Yeah."

I feel like that with my mom sometimes. I wish she would either make an effort or disappear for good. To come home after school and see the evidence of her presence: the sloshing sound of the dishwasher, the new air freshener installed in the hallway as you enter, an open magazine on the coffee table—it hurts more than it would if she just disappeared. At least then, I could move on and not hold out for her to change her mind and decide she wants a relationship with me.

"I'm sorry."

She grabs my hand. "I don't know what I'd do without you."

Squeezing her back, I reply, "I wish I could do more."

We slow at a stop light and Chloe switches on the radio

before tucking her long hair behind her ears. She's the spitting image of her mom, with the same almond-colored eyes, hazel hair and upturned nose. She always says she wishes she had honey-blonde hair like me. It makes no sense. I would love to have her hair color. I suppose we always want what we don't have.

Dylan waits for us as we arrive at school. We've barely exited the car when he pulls her in for a kiss. They've been together since they were fourteen, and it's a sweet relationship, but it's also an intense one. They're rarely apart, and Dylan is possessive. The girls at school swoon over him with his blonde, tousled hair and dimples. I don't know what it is about girls and their attraction to alphaholes.

"Willow, Willow, Willow," Dylan says in greeting because he knows it gets on my nerves.

"Dylan, Dylan, Dylan," I reply, pushing the car door shut and walking ahead.

Chloe giggles behind me, and it's all I can do not to roll my eyes. "Are you coming to the party tonight, Willow?" Dylan asks.

Winking at me, Chloe replies, "I'm not giving her a choice."

My heart softens. I would do anything to help Chloe keep her focus off her mother today. I know how hard this day is for her, and the last thing I want is for her to be alone. If she wants to drag me to a party, I'll put my antisocial tendencies aside for one night and suffer through it. I'll sit in a corner and pretend I'm blind to the drunk girls dancing on the tables and the boys doing a keg stand in the kitchen. I'll even pretend I'm having a good time. I can be an amazing actress when I want to be.

I smile at Dylan over my shoulder. "I'll be there."

"You know," he starts, walking ahead to open the door for us, "my friend, Luca, has the hots for you. I can introduce you to him."

I raise my brow but don't reply as I step into the crowded hallway. I'm not interested in his friends. They're all the same: fucking random girls and spending their free time riding their skateboards down at the park.

"Luca is nice," Chloe says to me as we make our way to our lockers.

"If you're into boys like that, sure," I reply drily, sidestepping a football player. Why are they all built like tanks?

We reach the lockers, and Chloe leans her shoulder against hers, studying me. "What's your type? We're seventeen, and you've never dated anyone."

Shrugging, I input my combination. "I don't think I have a type. The boys here bore me, that's all."

"You won't give anyone a chance." She opens her locker. "If you let Luca take you out, he might surprise you."

"How?"

"I don't know." She shuts her locker, zips up her bag, and shoulders it. "Maybe you have more in common than you think."

I humor her because the eagerness in her eyes is cute. "Like what?"

"Maybe you both like popcorn? Or maybe you both have an affinity for true crime? Maybe he's really funny?"

"Funny?" I shut my locker too, shouldering my bag. "Now *that* would be a surprise."

"You love that show… What's it called? Where they're stranded on an island?"

"Lost?"

"That's the one," she says as we start walking toward the classroom. "Maybe he likes it too?"

"Or maybe he doesn't."

"You won't know that unless you let him take you out." With a mischievous smile, she nudges my elbow, and I find myself chuckling.

"You're very adamant that I should give him a chance."

Pausing outside the classroom, she shrugs her shoulders. "I think you'll have a good time."

I reach up and flick her long ponytail. "I'm holding you personally responsible when I have the worst time of my life. You know, at the end of the night, when he tries to kiss me in his car, and we end up bumping noses instead? Yeah, you'll never hear the end of it. We'll turn thirty, and I'll still complain about that one time I let you talk me into going on a date with Luca."

Her beaming face makes the sacrifice worth it. If it keeps her smiling today, I'll let every boy at school bore me with their Star Wars talk.

"And I promise to always put you in uncomfortable positions that we can laugh about twenty years from now because that's what best friends do."

Laughing, we enter the classroom.

CHAPTER 2
WILLOW

MUSIC PLAYS from Chloe's speakers while she applies her blood-red lipstick in the mirror. I'm like a newborn lamb on ice as I step out of the adjoining bathroom in a pair of six-inch, black heels and a gold dress, which she insisted I try on. "I feel stupid."

She smacks her lips, fluffing her hair, then straightens up. Her excited squeal makes me wince. "You look amazing! Wow, look at your tits in that dress."

Swaying on my feet, I tug down on the fabric around my thighs. Well, I try to, but it barely covers my ass. "I look ridiculous."

"Don't be silly. You'll have every man drooling over you tonight."

Just then, there's a knock on the door, and Dylan enters the room. When he spots me, he does a double take. "Holy shit!"

"Right?" Chloe's tinkling laughter drifts on the heavy bass like a crowd-surfing rockstar. "Doesn't she look amazing?"

"Who knew you hid all that beneath your band T-shirts, Willow?"

I flip him off.

"Luca will be here soon. He's running five minutes late."

Walking over to the door, I throw a look at Chloe, who waves me off.

"Don't write him off just yet."

"I'm grabbing a beer. Do you guys want one?"

"Sure," Chloe replies, glancing at Dylan. "Do you want one?"

"Yeah, go on then. I'll have one."

I walk downstairs to the kitchen. Black, marble tiles meet dark-gray cupboards and a feature wall of exposed brick. The kitchen island in the middle always has a bowl of fruit filled with grapes and fresh red apples.

Opening the fridge, I find what I'm looking for. I remove three bottles of beer and shut the fridge.

"I really shouldn't turn a blind eye," Mr. Reid says, entering the kitchen.

Turning, I lean back against the fridge. "Probably not."

Mr. Reid looks rough today, with dark circles beneath his eyes, his tie hanging loose, and his buttons undone. It's as if he remains strong all year, but on this date—this one single day—he lets himself fall apart.

"Hand me one, please."

I do, watching him search a kitchen drawer for an opener. He pops the lid and brings the bottle to his lips, downing half of it in one go.

Swallowing thickly, I chew on my lip, unsure what to say. "I'm sorry."

It feels inadequate. Something lame you say to fill the silence, not to comfort or to soothe someone else but to make yourself less uncomfortable in the presence of palpable grief.

His tired eyes meet mine, and for a long moment, he simply looks at me, pinning me to the fridge door with his pain. "Look after my daughter tonight. Take her mind off all this and ensure she has a good time."

"I will," I promise.

His eyes slide down my body and then back up again. He clears his throat and takes another swig of his beer, not breaking eye contact. I can barely breathe when he looks at me that way, seeing but unseeing. I open my mouth to speak, to say something—anything—to break this awkward, tense silence, but I'm saved when the doorbell sounds.

Mr. Reid leaves the room, and I inhale a deep breath, my chest rising and falling in quick succession as I grip the counter behind me.

"Willow!" he calls out, deep and gravelly.

I place the drinks down, push off the counter and walk on unsteady legs into the hallway where Dylan's friend, Luca, looks uncomfortable beneath Mr. Reid's heavy stare.

"Hi." I gesture to the stairs. "I'll just let the others know that you're here."

I walk off before he can reply. The stairs creak as I ascend, in no hurry to make it to the top. Luca is good-looking with his short, black hair, dark eyes and olive skin, but that doesn't mean I'm interested in him.

When I open the bedroom door, I find Dylan on top of Chloe on her bed. Her red dress lies pooled around her hips, and her creamy thighs are wrapped around Dylan's waist. She moans into his mouth, not yet aware of my presence. I clear my throat, and she shoves him off like it's her father in the doorway instead of me. She quickly covers her breasts and her cheeks warm when she rights her clothes.

"Luca is here," I tell them.

Dylan discreetly adjusts his dick in his jeans before sliding past me.

Standing up, Chloe tucks her hair behind her ear. I'm tempted to point out that her lipstick is smeared. "So, are you ready to have fun?"

Hooking my arm in her elbow, we leave her room and descend the steps. Mr. Reid is still there, glaring at poor Luca. I think Chloe's dad has had an easy ride. He'll never warm completely to Dylan, but at least Chloe's boyfriend has stuck to his daughter for the last three years. Mr. Reid can rest assured at night that Dylan loves his daughter, even if he would have blown a gasket if he'd walked in on them five minutes ago.

Luca is new, and new boys awaken the protective side of Mr. Reid. I might not be his biological daughter, but Chloe's dad has known me since his daughter turned four and decided we should be best friends.

"Come on." With a hand on Chloe's lower back, Dylan leads her outside.

Luca clears his throat, glancing at Mr. Reid over my shoulder before his eyes return to me. "You look great."

I look stupid. "Thanks."

"Are you ready to go?"

Wetting my lips nervously, I nod. "Sure."

A part of me wishes Mr. Reid would forbid me from going. That way, I don't have to spend the entire evening making small talk with the boy in front of me. Unfortunately, I'm not Mr. Reid's daughter, so he says nothing.

We follow Chloe and Dylan to Luca's car. They take the backseat, and I reluctantly get in the front. What do people say on first dates? Is that what this is? A first date?

One look at my house tells me my mom is away, as always. The windows are dark except for the lamp in my bedroom window. Seeing it shine some light in the empty house makes me feel less alone.

❄

HIDING outside in the garden on one of the sun loungers, I stargaze. I make that sound like I'm alone. I'm not. The infinity pool is lined with girls in bikinis, despite the autumn chill, who shriek every time one of the boys cannonballs into the water.

Not only that, but Luca is here too, watching me on the sun lounger next to his. I suppose I should be pleased that he finds me interesting enough to stay by my side, but that would be a lie. I don't mind being alone.

"Where's Chloe?" I ask, looking around.

Luca takes a swig of his beer and shrugs. "They're probably up in one of the bedrooms."

It wouldn't surprise me. Three years later, they still fuck like rabbits.

"Do you want another beer?" Luca asks.

I look down at my empty cup. "No, I'm fine."

I really want to go home. I'm here for Chloe, but she disappeared as soon as we entered the house. Since then, I've put up with Luca's incessant talking.

"Why don't you go to the parties that much?"

"I don't enjoy them," I reply matter-of-factly. There's no point beating around the bush.

"I don't either," he admits with a shrug, and I look up.

"You don't?"

"No," he shakes his head, "not really. Dylan drags me along most of the time."

"Why do you let him?" Color me intrigued—he has sparked my interest.

His broad shoulders lift and fall as he sweeps his eyes over my face. "If you don't attend these parties, you stop being invited."

Now I'm confused. "So? Wouldn't that be a good thing?"

"Ya think? I don't want my friends to forget about me. They enjoy these parties, so I tag along. Isn't that why you're here tonight? Because Chloe wanted to come?"

"She's my best friend."

"Exactly."

My lips twitch. "You're a smartass."

That makes him smile and lean close with his elbows on

his thighs. "So are you." He sits back and crumples up his plastic cup. "Wanna get out of here?"

I pause, then blurt, "I'm not fucking you."

His eyes snap to mine, and for a long minute, he just stares. Laughter climbs up his throat, confusing me even more. "Damn, you say it straight."

"Well, yeah…"

"Is that what you thought I meant?"

My throat jumps. "It's code for 'let's go upstairs,' isn't it?"

He shakes his head before rising to his feet and holding his hand out. "Come on, let's go."

I debate for a brief moment about what to do. I'm not used to boys. Unlike Chloe, I don't want to date high school boys. The last thing I need is for Luca to get the wrong idea. Despite this, I take his hand and allow him to pull me to my feet.

He goes to speak, but raised voices interrupt what he was about to say.

"You fucking asshole! You thought I wouldn't find out?"

Luca and I exchange a glance as Chloe and Dylan burst through the patio doors.

"You're making this into something it's not!"

Chloe whirls on him and slaps him across the cheek. "Fuck you! So if a boy sent me nudes, it wouldn't be a big deal?"

"Where the fuck are you going?!" Dylan roars when she sets off down the side of the house.

We run after her too.

"Away from you!"

"The fuck you are!" Dylan pulls her to a stop.

"It's the anniversary of my mom's disappearance, Dylan," Chloe says with a broken voice. "Out of all the days to find out about this shit, it had to happen today." She swipes angrily at her cheeks.

"It didn't mean anything. They were just pictures."

The sadness in her eyes turns to fury. "Just pictures? Just fucking pictures?!"

"Yes! I never touched her."

"It doesn't fucking matter! You asked her for pictures and did what? Jerked off to them? Sexted her?"

Luca whispers in my ear, "Let me drive you home. I think they need to be alone."

My instincts tell me no. I don't want Chloe to be upset and alone tonight. Especially not now.

"I'm taking her home," Luca says, loudly enough for them to hear. "Is that okay?"

Chloe's red-rimmed eyes clash with mine and she wipes her cheeks before nodding. "Yes, please. I need to speak to Dylan. I'll ask Amanda or Jenny to drive me home."

"Are you sure? I can wait."

She shakes her head. "No, you go."

It still doesn't feel right, but I let Luca steer me toward his car. Before we turn the corner, I hear Chloe shout, "Don't touch me! It's over between us."

"The fuck it is! You think I'll let you go? You're overreacting."

Luca opens the door and guides me inside. I stare numbly at the house as he enters the car and pulls away from the curb. It really doesn't feel right to leave like this.

"They'll be fine."

I drag my eyes away from the passenger window. "How do you know?"

"They've fought before. They always end up back together."

"He's never done something like this before, though. Fighting over silly shit is not the same as finding nudes on your boyfriend's phone."

Luca winces. "He messed up big this time."

"You didn't know?"

Our eyes lock, and he frowns. "Why would I know?"

"Boys talk."

He blows out a breath as he flicks the blinker to turn right. "Not about this shit."

"So you didn't know he was cheating."

"No."

When we pull up outside my house, I look at my lap while I push down my cuticle with my nail. "I feel bad for leaving. What kind of a friend does that?"

Turning his body halfway, he replies, "They needed privacy. She'll be fine."

"You think?"

"Yeah."

I chew on my lip nervously as the silence presses on. I don't know what to say or do.

"I'll see you tomorrow," he says finally.

Releasing a relieved breath, I push open the car door and exit the vehicle. Before I leave, I lean down. "Thanks for the lift."

His lips spread in a barely-there, rueful smile. "Anytime."

I shut the door and make my way up the front steps of my house. The silence that greets me does little to ease my growing anxiety. Flicking on the hallway light, I toe off my heels, releasing a soft moan. Fuck, my feet hurt.

I fish my phone out of my bag and send a quick text to Chloe.

> Me: Message me when you get home so I know you're safe.

CHAPTER 3
WILLOW

I WAKE up to an insistent banging on the front door. My head hurts this morning after the beer I drank last night. I don't drink often, so it doesn't take much.

Tossing the quilt off, I throw my legs over the side of the bed and hurry downstairs. "I'm coming."

The banging continues, a hand smashing against the wood over and over again.

I unlock it and throw it open, coming face to face with a frantic Mr. Reid.

"Where is she? Is she with you?"

Before I can reply, he storms past me, his large steps carrying him down the hallway.

"What's wrong? Mr. Reid?" I chase after him, but he's already upstairs. The floor creaks beneath his heavy steps. I take chase, running up the staircase. "Mr. Reid?"

I find him in my bedroom, where he stands, staring at the crumpled sheets on my bed.

"Where's Chloe?"

I stiffen.

He turns around and looks at me pleadingly. "Please tell me she's here."

I don't know what to say. "No, I left before her last night. She was catching a ride back with Amand—"

He strides past me, rushing down the stairs. I can barely keep up. "What's wrong? What's happened to Chloe?"

He doesn't reply, and the panic inside me grows.

"Mr. Reid?!"

I chase him outside into the overcast, early morning. Pulling him to a stop, I step in front of him. "Where's Chloe?"

The fight seems to leave him. Dressed in gray joggers and a white T-shirt, he looks exhausted. I'm suddenly aware of my tiny sleep shorts and tank top. The chill in the air makes my nipples harden against the thin fabric.

Mr. Reid is too worried to pay any attention to my state of undress. "She never returned home last night."

"She probably stayed over at Dylan's."

They must have made up in the end. It's what they do.

"She always messages me to tell me her plans." He walks off toward his house.

I follow hot on his heels. "Maybe she forgot this time."

He stops at the door and grips the handle, inhaling a steadying breath. His jaw tightens and a muscle ticks in his cheek. "Will you phone Dylan for me, please?"

"Of course. I'll phone him now."

I walk back to my house, feeling strangely numb. The fear in Mr. Reid's eyes was real, and it's infectious.

Hurrying up the steps to my room, I make a beeline for my phone on the nightstand.

> Me: Message me when you get home so I know you're safe.

The message was marked as seen, but she never replied.

My fingers tremble as I bring up Dylan's number. It takes me a few attempts, but I finally succeed. Pressing the phone to my ear, I wait with bated breath.

He answers on the third ring, his voice croaky. "Hello?"

"Dylan?"

"Who's this?" He's in his bed. I can hear him shifting beneath his sheets.

"It's Willow. Is Chloe with you?"

His deep voice breathes out, "No. She walked home alone last night."

I grow cold. "What? Why didn't she catch a lift with someone?"

"You know how stubborn she is sometimes."

"What about Amanda? Jenny?"

His sleepy voice sounds in my ear. "Look, I don't know. She was angry with me and decided to walk home."

"And you let her?!" I almost shriek. "Why, Dylan? Why would you let her walk home alone?"

"We were both fucking angry, okay? What was I supposed to do? Manhandle her?"

My eyes catch on Mr. Reid's bedroom window across from mine. He's pacing the small space.

"Willow?" Dylan's voice brings me back to the here and now.

"She's missing," I breathe out in a weak, shaky voice.

"What?" He's more alert now. I can practically hear his frown.

"She never came home last night."

Dylan remains silent, breathing down the line.

"She never came home, Dylan," I repeat, my voice breaking.

"Shit," he whispers, and there's rustling in the background. "I'll make some phone calls to see if anyone saw anything last night."

"I'll be over in a bit. Let's look for her together."

He hangs up, and I drop down on my bed. Resting my elbows on my thighs, I bury my face in my hands. What the fuck am I going to do? What *can* I do?

I lift my head and look to my left. Mr. Reid has left his bedroom. How do I tell him that she didn't go back with Dylan?

My heart aches as I make my way back to his house. I enter and find him in the kitchen, talking to someone on the phone.

When he looks up and spots me, he holds his finger up. "I'll have to phone you back, okay? Willow is here."

He hangs up, watching me expectantly as if I'm the only one who can put him out of his misery. My heart splinters at the hopeful look in his eyes. I'm about to crush it.

I open my mouth, but no words come out. Nothing at all.

"I'm sorry," I eventually croak.

Mr. Reid looks at me uncomprehendingly for such a long moment that my heart starts to pound against my ribcage. Each individual heartbeat smashes against its confines. It roars in my ear, eating up the silence in the room.

"She wasn't at Dylan's."

"She wasn't at Dylan's," he repeats quietly to himself, chewing on his thumbnail. His brain is desperately trying to piece it all together. "Who took her home?"

"She walked home alone."

His dark eyes clash with mine and his raw voice crackles with pain. "You let her walk home alone?"

"No," I reply, confused as to why he would say such a thing. "She told me she would catch a lift with Amanda or Jenny."

"You let her walk home alone!" he repeats, louder this time while walking closer and forcing me back a step.

"She promised me she would be okay."

"SHE ISN'T FUCKING OKAY!" he roars, and I whimper with fear when he corners me against the wall. "Where the fuck is my daughter, Willow?! You're her best friend. I trusted you to keep her safe."

"I-I tried to stay. She didn't want me to."

He slaps the wall, making my heart jump to my throat. "She's missing! All because you decided to leave her side."

"I'm sorry." My voice is weak and pitiful.

His harsh breaths fan my face while he glares at me as if it's a struggle to rein in his anger, his pain. He's been here before, five years ago when his wife went missing. Now he's here again, experiencing the same thing, battling the same fear. It's palpable in the air, coaxing my own out to dance with his.

Stepping back, he runs a hand down his face. "I'm calling the police."

"She could be with someone else. Maybe she stayed over with another friend?"

He's already typing away on his phone. His eyes never leave mine while he talks to the call handler, and I make no move to leave. I would rather he direct his fury at me than go through this nightmare alone. Chloe is my best friend... I should have stayed with her last night. It was fucking foolish of me to think I could leave her on her own. That's not what best friends do. They stay.

He hangs up, and the silence presses in once again, making it hard to breathe. I can understand why Mr. Reid is jumping to conclusions after his previous experience with his wife disappearing. But why am I? Chloe could be anywhere. Maybe she went back to the party and stayed with Amanda. Maybe she thought 'Fuck this' and took a bus somewhere. Maybe she just wanted time alone.

"You should leave."

"But Chloe—"

"I'll tell you if the police find her."

"Oh."

He grinds his teeth, gazing out the window.

As the silence presses on, I walk out, unable to breathe until I'm safely locked away in my own house. Pressing my back against the door, I release a sob, slamming my hand over my mouth. Pain lances through me. I lower my hand and take a few steadying breaths. In through my nose and out through my mouth.

The police will find her. She's with a friend, that's all. I'll soon awaken from this nightmare.

CHAPTER 4
WILLOW
NOVEMBER 3RD, 2015

THE HOUSE IS SILENT, as always, when I walk downstairs in the early evening to grab something to eat. Chloe has been missing for a week.

Seven long days without her here.

Mr. Reid has since gone live on TV to plead for his daughter's safe return. There's even a reward of ten thousand dollars to anyone with information that leads to a break in the case.

Walking into the kitchen, I switch on the small TV on the counter before opening the fridge. We don't have much in the house, but that's nothing new. I reach for the leftover pasta salad from yesterday, then pause, listening.

"Dylan Cooper from the small town of Skelton was arrested earlier this evening in connection with the murder of high school student Chloe Reid."

I shut the fridge and stare at the TV.

Murder? Dylan killed her?

"There is still no body in the case of the missing high school girl who disappeared in the early hours of the twenty-seventh of October, but police believe they have sufficient evidence to charge Chloe's

boyfriend, Dylan, with her murder. Blood matching Chloe's was found in his bedroo—"

Switching off the TV, I place the remote on the counter. I'm trembling. The silence threatens to suffocate me, and I blink against the tears that sting the backs of my eyes.

"Oh my god…"

My feet move, carrying me out of the kitchen and into the hallway. I put on my Chucks before hurrying outside. It's drizzling with rain, and by the time I've crossed the grass to Mr. Reid's porch, my hair is frizzy, and my gray Oxford hoodie is damp. I knock on the door and wait. I don't know what I want to say to Mr. Reid. I just know that I don't want to be alone right now.

The lock sounds in the door and then it opens, revealing Mr. Reid. He's unshaven, with bloodshot eyes and a food stain on his white T-shirt. I've never seen him this unkempt before. He used to take pride in his looks, but losing his daughter…

"I watched the news."

He opens the door further and steps aside, a silent invitation for me to enter.

"Can I get you anything?" he asks in a croaky voice. I quickly shake my head, following him into the living room, where we take a seat on the couch. The coffee table is littered with empty pizza boxes and beer bottles. There's even an ashtray with cigarette stubs. I've never seen Mr. Reid smoke in my life.

"I don't know how to feel," he admits. "Relieved that someone was arrested? Sad because they believe she was murdered?" He scoffs, elbows on knees.

"Both?" I suggest softly. I've never lost a family member. I can't begin to imagine the pain Mr. Reid is going through right now. I feel lost without my best friend.

"Fuck," he breathes out, rubbing his face. "I always thought Dylan was a decent guy."

When he looks at me, tears bead on his lashes. I don't reply because I don't know what to say. Mr. Reid seems happy not to be alone. We sit in silence, both deep in our own thoughts.

"Can they arrest him when the only evidence is blood?" I ask him.

"Yeah."

"What if he didn't do it?"

Mr. Reid sighs long and deep. "We have to trust that the investigators know what they're doing. Dylan was the last one to be seen with her. Her blood was in his bedroom."

I chew my lip. It's hard to imagine Dylan would ever hurt Chloe, but he was sometimes jealous and possessive.

"How are you holding up?"

Tucking my hair behind my ear, I attempt to steady my shaky inhale. "I miss her."

He stays silent, waiting for me to carry on.

"She came around every morning, you know?" My vision blurs. When I blink, tears fall, and I wipe them away. "It's so quiet now. I keep expecting her to walk into my house every morning. She never knocked." I release a soft laugh. "She just waltzed right in like she owned the place."

Inhaling a ragged breath, I whisper, "Mr. Reid—"

He shakes his head. "Call me Grayson."

"Grayson." I taste the letters on my tongue. "She could still be alive."

His beard rasps as he drags his fingers through it. "I want to believe it so badly, but the evidence is telling us otherwise. The police changed it to a murder investigation the day after her disappearance. It's not an abduction, Willow. I'm sorry."

I don't like that he's apologizing to me. His daughter is missing because I left the party early. It's my fault he looks like a shell of his former self.

I leave him on the couch and walk into his kitchen, where

I reach for the garbage bags in the cupboard beneath the sink. Grabbing the roll, I tear one off and shake it out.

Grayson is where I left him, staring blankly out the window when I return. His eyes skate over to me as I clear his coffee table. "What are you doing?"

"You can't live like this."

"I'll tidy it up later."

I don't stop cleaning. Not until his coffee table is empty of pizza boxes and beer cans. I even throw out the entire ashtray. The room stinks, so I open a window to let in some fresh air. It smells of drizzling rain and trees. Breathing it in, I slowly turn. Grayson rolls his head on the back of the couch and stares at me for a long moment. "It's hard to look at you."

"Why?"

A car drives past outside. I watch it park in a driveway further down the street.

"You and my daughter were inseparable. From the moment you became friends, you were always together."

"Not recently," I point out, my throat clogged with emotion.

Grayson lifts his shoulders and lets them fall. "That's teenage love for you. I remember how intense it got at times."

"I wouldn't know," I reply, scanning the room. It's decorated in gray and white with yellow accents. It's modern but also homely.

Grayson doesn't reply. He simply sighs and stares at the ceiling as if it holds the answers he needs to locate his daughter.

"Do you want me to get you anything from the shop, Grayson? Maybe some milk?"

"How can time move so slowly?"

"Because you're waiting," I reply, and he looks at me again. "Time always drags when you want something to happen."

His throat jumps, but he stays silent, and I take that as my cue to leave. Tying up the garbage bag, I exit the room. The walls in the hallway are lined with photographs of Chloe at various stages in her life: ballet competitions, her first visit from the tooth fairy, the time we dressed up as mermaids. Her eyes follow me as I walk past. I shake off the shiver that crawls down my spine.

CHAPTER 5
WILLOW
DECEMBER 5TH, 2015

I RAISE my hand to knock on Grayson's door but lower it again, chewing on my lip. I don't want to bother him, but I haven't seen him in weeks. He's still off work, hiding away in his house. I want to feel close to Chloe again. I just need to be in her home for an hour. Sit at her table and pretend for five seconds that she's coming back.

That everything is normal.

Steadying my nerves, I knock.

The door opens with a creak, revealing the ghost of a man who's lost everything. I thought that maybe he would have gone back to work by now, or at least attempted a walk outside in the sun, but he has completely retreated into himself. My eyes slide down his creased, gray T-shirt, black joggers that hang low on his hips, and bare feet. Hugging the paper bag filled with groceries to my chest, I clear my throat. "Can I come in?"

"Why are you here, Willow?" he asks, sounding tired and defeated.

"You never leave the house." I hesitate, then add, "I brought groceries."

The door opens the rest of the way, and Grayson walks

ahead, disappearing down the hallway. I scan my eyes across the empty street before entering the house and closing the door. The blinds are drawn; it's dark. "Grayson?"

I find him sitting at the kitchen table, staring at nothing. He looks like he hasn't slept in weeks.

"I thought I could cook us something to eat." I place the bag on the counter and unpack it, softly placing the items down. I don't want to startle him or make him feel uncomfortable in his own home. The silence that follows is only disturbed by the ruffling of the paper bag.

"I don't know what you like to eat, so I bought a range of items."

After packing away the milk, eggs and bread, I unearth a chopping board in one of the cupboards. Grayson says nothing while I chop the onion in silence or when I start to fry the pieces. Sprinkling more oil in the pan, I reach for the minced garlic. It fizzles loudly. Using a wooden spatula, I separate the meat. "I hope you like spaghetti Bolognese." I don't tell him that I know he does. Mrs. Reid cooked it for Chloe and me when we had sleepovers involving face masks and Disney movies.

When he doesn't respond, I talk for no other reason than to fill the silence. "I've been back at school for the last two weeks. It's not the same, you know? The gossip has died down until the trial. At least there's that. I still can't get over that Dylan did it... They were the golden couple."

Silence descends again while I pour in the chopped tomatoes and give it a good stir. My heart is in my throat, thumping heavily.

"The house is so fucking quiet," he whispers.

My breath catches, and I pause stirring the Bolognese.

"I just want her to come back and make some fucking noise. Play her Taylor Swift album full blast. Smoke cigarettes with her window open, thinking I won't notice." His raw chuckle breaks my heart. "I always noticed. You girls weren't discreet. I just chose not to give you a hard time for being teenagers."

"I'm sorry, Mr. Reid."

"It's Grayson."

"Grayson," I whisper. "I miss her too."

Rising from his seat, he joins me at the counter, reaching for a pan in the cupboard. He fills it with water and puts it on the stove. We prepare the food in silence. It's comfortable. Peaceful, even.

When the pasta is boiling and the Bolognese is simmering, he leans back against the counter. I feel his eyes on me, but I don't meet his gaze as I rinse the chopping board and knife.

"Thank you for this. Grief is a dark and lonely place sometimes."

"You don't have to be alone with your feelings."

Grayson changes the subject. "How's your mom? I haven't seen her in a while."

That makes two of us. I switch the tap off and place the chopping board on the dish rack. After drying my hands, I take a seat at the kitchen table. Grayson joins me. "I'm sure she's fine."

"She leaves you alone a lot, doesn't she?"

"It's like she's never there," I admit. "It sucks. I was always envious of Chloe. She had a loving family who turned up for every school show and every ballet competition. Even when your wife disappeared, you still showed up. Chloe was never alone. I don't think my mom turned up to a single event."

Grayson rubs the back of his neck. "I had no idea it was that bad."

"No one notices," I reply, stroking my fingers over the tablecloth. "Mom, she…" I clear my throat. "She feeds me, washes my clothes, keeps the house clean and the lawn mowed. People only start to notice the neglect when the grass grows, the dishes pile high, and the weight starts falling off."

My eyes flit up to his. "It's why I knocked on your door tonight. I don't want to be alone all the time. Now that Chloe is gone, I…"

"I know," he replies softly.

"I have no one. I'm not like Chloe, who had lots of friends. Now that she's gone, no one knocks on my door."

That's the thing about grief—it alienates you from others. It's a disease. Once it digs its claws into you, everyone else gives you a wide berth. I'm now the girl with the dead best friend, and no one at school wants to associate with death.

Grayson's chair scrapes on the floor. I watch in silence while he pours the water out of the pan and plates our food. His house smells of a home-cooked meal for once instead of pizza, beer, and misery. Almost as if a tendril of warmth has seeped through the floorboards to ward off the darkness.

We eat in silence. That's the thing about grief, too—it doesn't need conversation. It doesn't speak in words. Its language is subtle, gentle even. Haunted eyes, a shared look, a weak smile. It is heavy sighs and wishing you could fill the silence but not having the strength to try. That's me now, hunting for a subject to chase away our grief.

He speaks first. "This tastes so much better than pizza and microwave meals."

His words have me blossoming like a flower in spring. "You like it?"

Nodding, he says, "It's the first home-cooked meal I've had since…"

And there it is, creeping back out from the shadows to steal the glimmer of light from his eyes, snatching it away like a thief in the night.

"We should make it a thing."

His fork scrapes against the plate. "A thing?"

"You know?" I say with a shrug. "Eat together a few times a week. My mom is away, and you're here alone. I think it would mean a lot to Chloe if we tried to honor her in some way." My eyes dance across the kitchen, the soft light from the lamp in the window, the photographs and school letters attached to the fridge with magnets. "I feel close to her here. I remember the time we decided to bake scones. When Chloe grabbed the bag of flour, the bottom split. You would think it all poured to the floor and that was it, but no," I chuckle softly, circling my fork in the pasta, "it was a cloud of flour."

"I remember," Grayson says with a soft smile, the first one I've seen since his daughter's disappearance. "You looked like ghosts with your faces covered in white flour, and your hair…" he trails off, shoulders dancing with amusement. "Your eyes popped wide open when I walked into the kitchen."

"I always liked that about you, Grayson. You never got mad."

Not unlike my mom, who can't stand a mess. The only time she engages in conversation is when she shouts at me. Sometimes I deliberately do stuff I shouldn't to get her attention, even if it's only for her to call me useless and remind me of what a mistake it was to keep me.

"It would take a cold heart to get mad at you girls. You always got into some crazy situations."

We share a smile, and my heart begins to feel warm and fuzzy when I recall Chloe's infectious laughter.

"I should go." Standing up, I collect the dishes and bring them to the sink, then proceed to wash and dry them. I don't want to leave Grayson with a mess, not when I invited myself here.

When I turn around, he stands up too. "Want to do this again soon?" I ask, expecting him to turn me down while desperately hoping he won't.

"I'd love that."

CHAPTER 6
WILLOW
JANUARY 3RD, 2016

AS THE WEEKS PASS, Grayson and I meet up several more times to cook together and exchange memories of Chloe. I don't know if it helps him, but every time I succeed in drawing a smile from his lips or lifting the darkness in his gaze—if only for a short moment—my own soul feels lighter somehow. It's my way of making up for not walking Chloe home that night. I can't shift the guilt, no matter how hard I try.

I'm standing outside my local convenience store, staring at a photograph of Dylan in an orange jumpsuit on the front page of a newspaper.

"Trial set for April," I whisper, reading the headline.

The bell sounds above the door as a middle-aged woman with curly hair and caked-on makeup steps outside. After lighting a cigarette and inhaling the smoke deep into her lungs, she says on the exhale, "He was eighteen at the time of the murder."

I drag my eyes away from his photograph and peer at her in the afternoon sun. The embers crackle as she takes another drag. She blows the smoke out to the side, regarding me, before tipping her chin at the newspaper. "He's eligible for the death penalty."

My heart lurches in my chest. She must notice my discomfort because she steps out of the way as the door to the store opens again. She moves closer. "Was he your friend?"

Her southern twang is strong. It's soothing, like a warm hug on a cold autumn morning. "The girl who died… Chloe…" I clear my throat. "She was my best friend."

"Oh, darling." The cigarette is back between her pink lips, and she squints as she inhales.

I look back at the image. Dylan looks like a shell of his former self.

"He'll be getting hell in there."

A lump forms in my throat as her words register. "I thought they kept them separated?"

"They will, darling. Once he gets sentenced."

"They could still drop the death penalty and pursue a hefty sentence."

"They could," she agrees, taking one final suck on her cancer stick before crushing it under her heel. "But they won't."

My throat thickens even more, and I set off walking before I do something stupid like cry in front of a stranger. How is Dylan holding up in prison, knowing he might never get out? He had his whole world ahead of him, but now…

"Willow," a deep voice calls out behind me, and I turn. Grayson is walking toward me with two grocery bags in his hands.

My eyes widen and I motion at him with my hand. "You're outside in the sunshine."

He lifts his bags slightly. "A man's got to eat."

"I like your clothes," I blurt because it's true. It's the first time I've seen him in anything other than creased T-shirts and sweatpants in weeks.

Grayson looks down at his jeans and his ironed, navy-blue

shirt beneath his unzipped, black winter coat. The first top two buttons are undone, revealing a hint of chest. "Well, the T-shirt I wore this morning had a tomato stain. I decided it was time to shower and shave."

I'm smiling up at him. "I'm happy for you."

His lips twitch before he seems to catch himself. He lifts the bags again. "I figured it's my turn to cook for you."

"Yeah?" Something flutters in my belly.

"I can't let you do all the cooking."

"What did you have in mind?" I want to keep him talking. I don't know if it's the winter sunshine or what, but he seems brighter today.

"It'll be a surprise for later. If I tell you, and you say you don't like it—well, I'm not going back to the grocery store. Once is enough for today.

"Okay." My smile is soft.

Grayson half turns. "Want to come back to my house now or swing by later?"

I have no other plans, so I fall in step with him. We walk in silence, but it's comfortable silence. It's the kind I could bask in forever. It's a space where thoughts are allowed to coexist in peace.

"How's school?"

We cross the road. It's a short walk to our street from here.

"It's school, you know? Ever since Chloe disappeared, I haven't been able to focus."

"You shouldn't fall behind."

"I know," I reply, my arm brushing up against his. "I guess I struggle to see the importance now that I know how fragile life is. Chloe is gone, and I'm somehow supposed to care about calculus?"

"I get it." I like that Grayson talks to me like I'm an adult, not a child his daughter's age. "I have to return to work soon, and I lie awake at night, wondering how the fuck I'm supposed to move on."

I sense he wants to say more, so I wait for him to carry on.

"After my wife… At least I had Chloe back then. Because of her, I had no other choice but to stay strong. This time, I'm alone."

The path has been salted overnight, and the crunching underfoot is the only sound while we walk in silence. Grayson's house is just up ahead.

"You have to be strong for yourself," I reply when we reach his driveway. "Life carries on whether we want it to or not."

"You know," he says as he puts his bags down on the porch, digging in his pockets for the house keys, "you're very mature for your age."

"So are you."

That makes him laugh, and the sound tugs at my heartstrings. "I would hope so at my age."

We enter the house and Grayson makes a beeline for the kitchen, where he proceeds to unload the bags on the kitchen counter. I walk to his living room and peruse the pictures of Chloe on the mantelpiece. I can't imagine how hard it is to sit in here every night with her ghost in the room.

Grayson eventually joins me with a beer in his hand. He holds out a glass of lemon water, which I gratefully accept.

"I remember when you took this picture." I point to a photograph of Chloe and me at the town hall when we went to our first concert. It was only a local band, but we were super excited anyway.

Grayson leans in, studying the photograph. His masculine scent settles in my nostrils before he moves back again. "You were thirteen or something, right?"

"Fourteen," I correct him.

Chuckling, he brings the rim of his beer to his lips and takes a swig while I watch his throat jump. I've always noticed Grayson in a way I don't notice the boys at school. I don't know if it's because he's always been in my life, more of a parent than my own absent mother. If I hurt myself, it was Grayson who cleaned my wounds and told me everything would be okay. When the kids at school were mean to me, it was Grayson who told me to keep my head high. Maybe that's why my eyes slide over the broad shoulders beneath his shirt. I quickly avert my gaze when he lowers the bottle and drags his tongue over the droplets on his bottom lip.

He walks up to the couch and lowers himself down, but I stay by the fireplace. I need space to calm my racing heart.

"So," Grayson says with a smile, "how do you feel about Butter Chicken and rice?"

"Is that what you're cooking?"

"It is."

He doesn't take his eyes off me when I approach him. "It sounds delicious."

"It is," he repeats, holding my gaze as I take a seat on the armchair.

"I look forward to trying it." I don't know what else to say. The way Grayson is watching me makes me feel flustered.

"Tell me something about you, Willow. What do you want to do in the future?"

"You're asking deep questions."

"It's an important one." Leaning back, he peels back the corner of the label. "I don't think I ever asked Chloe. I was always so hell-bent on letting her forge her own path. My father... he was never like that. He was always on my case, trying to steer me in a certain direction. It didn't go well. I never tried to push Chloe, but now I think I should have asked her..." A muscle jumps in his cheek, and he takes another swig of his beer. "I should have asked her what her dreams were."

The light in his eyes dims again, so I inhale a shaky breath and reply honestly, "I don't know what my dreams are."

The muscle in his jaw ticks again. Leaning forward, he puts the beer on the table. "You have time to find a dream."

"Maybe." To lighten the mood, I add, "I want to visit Paris one day."

He smiles at me, then claps his thighs and stands up. "I know it's early, but I'll start on the food. Do you want to watch a movie or something in the meantime?"

"Do you mind if I keep you company?"

"I'll teach you the recipe if you want."

I stand up too and follow him into the kitchen. After I finish my glass of lemon water, I rinse it out and put it on the drying rack.

CHAPTER 7
GRAYSON

I SHOULDN'T ENJOY her company like this. A young woman like Willow should be out with her friends, enjoying life. Not cooking food with a middle-aged man like me. But for whatever reason, she seems to want to be here. I enjoy the break in the silence. Willow talks a lot about everything and nothing. Sometimes she talks because she wants to fill the silence, and sometimes she talks simply to coax a smile from my lips. She's like a candle in the darkness. If not for her, I would be wasting away on my couch, staring at the unlit fireplace. At least while Willow is here, I get a short break from wallowing in my misery. I can see why Chloe liked her so much. She's witty but also sensitive. Young but also wise, thanks to her absent mom, who doesn't care beyond keeping her clothed and fed.

It's not enough. Willow craves company. She craves to be seen.

Our fingers brush as we reach for the knife at the same time. I pretend I don't notice her blushing cheeks. "You can have it. I'll grab another one."

Why am I encouraging her like this? I've always known she has an innocent crush on me, but I still don't turn her away. I don't want to when the alternative is to be alone, letting the pain back in. This is a nice distraction. Maybe that makes me a terrible person, but nothing will ever happen between us. She's my daughter's age, not even legal yet.

My mouth moves before my brain has caught up. "Your eighteenth birthday is shortly after Chloe's, right?"

Why am I asking her this? It doesn't matter.

"Yeah, but I don't think I'll do much this year."

"You're weeks away from turning eighteen. Of course, you should celebrate."

Instead of replying, she starts sautéing the onions and the chicken. My eyes snag on her bare shoulders in her tank top and the curve of her creamy neck when she tucks her hair behind her ear. "You should host a party," I say to distract myself from my hardening dick. This is bad, so fucking bad.

Those slender shoulders rise and fall noncommittally, and I find myself wondering if she's a virgin. I squash those thoughts immediately and set the table while she continues cooking.

"Where do you keep the ginger and the cumin?"

"In the top cupboard to your left."

She pushes up on her tiptoes, and my eyes land on her pert ass in those tight jeans before sliding down her long legs.

I quickly look back up when she turns and says, "Thanks."

When the dinner is cooked, and we're seated at the table, she steals my breath with a drawn-out moan as she tastes the food.

"This is… Wow, Grayson! I love it."

"That good, huh?"

She moans again, and I try my fucking hardest to keep my thoughts out of the gutter. It has clearly been too long since I got laid, and I'm projecting it on my dead daughter's best friend. That thought is the bucket of ice-cold water I need to clear my head.

"I don't think I can top this," she says, covering her mouth with her hand when she talks.

"Yeah?" I stand up and grab another beer from the fridge. After popping the lid, I take a swig while watching her. She has almost cleaned her plate. Nodding her head, she drags her thumb through the sauce before bringing it to her mouth. "It's delicious."

"Who taught you to cook?"

She shrugs, sucking the tip of her thumb clean. "I taught myself. There's never anyone home, you know? Chloe always liked to bake, so I also learned some things from her."

It makes sense. I've had to clean countless messes over the years after they decided to try a new recipe they found online. At least it filled the house with giggles and nice smells after my wife's disappearance.

"Did you buy dessert?" she asks when I continue watching her. I don't miss the hitch in her breath.

"There's ice cream in the fridge."

She makes no move to stand. Instead, she chews on her lip, seemingly in thought. "How about you, Grayson?"

The soft tone of her voice has me raising my brow.

She continues, "You asked me earlier what my dreams are. I know it's too soon since... well, since Chloe's disappearance, but you can't stay locked away in your house forever. What's your plan?"

Pushing off the fridge, I walk to the kitchen counter and stare at my reflection in the window while I take a swig of beer. The dark has long since settled, and the chill seeps in through the gaps in the window frame. It's a cold evening outside. "The frosty nights make it harder. I can't stop thinking, 'What if her body is dumped somewhere? What if she's cold?'"

The chair scrapes on the floor and then I feel her behind me, her soft breaths heating my left shoulder blade through the thin fabric of my shirt. She's close, too close.

"You can't let your thoughts go there, Mr. Reid. You'll torture yourself."

I turn, slowly placing my empty beer bottle down on the counter. "It's Grayson."

The air crackles between us as she wets her lips and offers a nervous smile. A smile I should not soak up with my eyes.

"I should go," she whispers.

"Yeah," I agree, dipping my gaze to her cleavage before looking away, "you should."

Her footsteps retreat, but before she leaves the kitchen, she turns in the doorway with her hand on the frame. "Thanks again for dinner."

Then she's gone, and I drop my head back between my shoulders, dragging a hand down my face. "Jesus Christ."

CHAPTER 8
WILLOW
JANUARY 13TH, 2016

I TEST the temperature of the water in the bathtub. It's bordering on too hot, which is just how I like it. If it's perfect, it cools down too soon.

As I step out of the adjoining bathroom and into my bedroom, I pause, gazing through the window. Grayson sits on the edge of his bed, staring straight forward with his elbows on his knees, fingers steepled in front of his mouth. I wonder what's going through his head.

My feet move deeper into the room. I turn in front of my bed, about to reach for the towel and clean clothes, when I hesitate. One look in the mirror on my bedroom door confirms it: Grayson has turned his head, his gaze burning my back.

I look down at the neatly-folded, crisp towel on top of my made bed. Everything is just so fucking perfect. Pink, flowery, and feminine. There's none of the darkness that I feel swirling in my belly as his brown eyes take me in. I shouldn't tempt a grown man, my dead best friend's father. I know better.

It doesn't stop me from hooking my fingers in the hem of my tank top and sliding it up and over my head.

It falls to the floor by my feet.

Reaching behind me, I hold my breath as I unclip my bra. It slides down my arms, and my nipples pebble as I imagine him watching me through his window. I don't dare look up in case our eyes catch in my mirror.

With trembling hands, I hook my thumbs in my sleep shorts and shimmy out of them. As they pool around my feet, I do the same to my lace panties. Straightening up, I suppress a whimper. My body tingles everywhere, hyperaware of his roaming eyes. I can't believe I'm doing this—standing naked before Chloe's father, pretending I don't know he's watching me.

I know.

I feel it.

Heat pools between my legs and my nipples ache to be tweaked and pulled. If he were here behind me, I would hold my breath, anticipating the brush of his touch over my soft skin.

I grab my things and make my escape to the bathroom. As soon as the door shuts, I lean back against the hard wood and drag in a shaky breath. What the heck is Grayson doing to me? I'm a good girl. I don't lust over middle-aged men or strip naked when I know they're watching me.

Only, I *am* that girl.

And I loved every second of it.

The bath water burns my skin as I climb in and sink below the rippling surface. I can't stop picturing Grayson in his bedroom. Is he touching himself? Stroking his big cock to thoughts of me? Is he imagining me naked on his bed, on all fours, begging him to fuck me?

My fingers slip beneath the surface and cup my heavy, achy breasts. Releasing a moan, I crane my neck back and let my eyes fall closed. Pleasure lights up my body as I roll my peaked nipples, pinching them hard.

"That's it, baby girl, let me hear how good I make you feel."

I whimper, trailing my fingers further down, over my

tensing stomach, and lower still until a gasp parts my lips. Sensation explodes as I press down on my swollen clit. The water ripples around me while I begin to circle my sensitive bundle of nerves. Lightly at first but then with more pressure. I make a keening sound I've never heard before. I touch myself when I'm alone—I'm no saint—but I don't recall ever being this worked up before. I could practically feel Grayson's eyes on me like a soft caress as I stood naked by my bedside. I didn't have to look up to know he'd gotten to his feet and moved closer to the window. I sensed it as surely as the journey his eyes took down my trembling body.

And I knew...

I knew if I looked up, I would see the same desire reflected in his dark eyes.

"Grayson," I moan, sliding a finger inside my tight pussy. The slight stretch feels amazing. How would it feel to be fingered by Grayson? His thick digits, stretching me wide in preparation for his hard dick?

My nipples resurface, pointy and hard, as I arch my back. I shove a second finger inside my tight warmth.

"That's my good girl. You'll take everything I give you."

My chest heaves, my legs spread wider, pressing against the bathtub's edge, and my fingers slide out to rub at my clit almost frantically while I tweak my nipples with my free hand. I need to get off. I'm so close. The water splashes over the sides, but I'm too lost to notice.

"Oh god, oh god," I whimper, biting down on my bottom lip. My pussy contracts and pleasure floods through me, tensing every muscle in my body.

"Grayson!"

My loud moans echo in the bathroom. Out of breath and spent, I slide down further beneath the surface until the rippling water sloshes against my chin. My clit tingles with aftershocks.

Submerging myself completely, I hold my breath until my lungs burn.

How am I going to face Grayson now?

❆

A WEEK LATER, I pause as I step into the kitchen to get a bite to eat. Mom is wiping down the already-pristine kitchen counter. Her blonde hair is up in a tight chignon, and her knee-length skirt and suit jacket are free of creases. She knows I'm here but doesn't acknowledge me as I step deeper into the room, wondering what I ever did to deserve her cold shoulder. Why she hates me so much that she won't even look at me.

"Mom?" I slide the chair out at the island. She continues wiping.

Tears bead in my eyes the longer she ignores me. "Mom?" I try again, but she puts the cloth down on the drying rack and shuts the cupboard to her right before walking out without another word.

The front door slams shut shortly after.

I release a shaky breath, and the tears blurring my vision spill over, trailing down my cheeks. I quickly wipe them off with my sleeve, then dig in my jeans pocket for my phone.

> Me: Message me when you arrive home so I know you're safe.

My fingers move over the screen before I swipe away more tears from my cheeks.

> Me: I miss you. I miss you so fucking much.

An automatic message pops up, notifying me that the message failed to send. My lip begins to tremble, and my eyes burn as I continue staring at the screen. She truly is gone. I know she is, but a small part of me still can't accept it. How long will grief have a tight hold on me? When will I stop listening for her laughter and expecting my phone to buzz with an incoming text?

She's never going to reply to my latest message.

Pocketing my phone, I jump off the chair and leave the kitchen, walking toward the front door. I need fresh air. I need to get out of this silent house.

The late afternoon sun is nowhere to be seen. Instead, it's a cold, gray winter's day. The thin layer of snow on the sidewalk, which began to melt after lunchtime, is now icing over. I'm on my porch, rubbing my hands together and blowing on them to keep warm, when a taxi pulls up outside of Grayson's house. With my heart in my throat, I watch him exit with a beautiful woman in tow. I can't take my eyes off her long, amber hair, flushed cheeks, and green wrap coat as he smiles at her while unlocking the front door.

They disappear inside his house, and I stand there for a long moment, unaware of the cold that seeps through my thin clothes. My fingers begin to tingle and I soon lose feeling in my toes. I'm torn from my stasis when a car speeds by, and a guy sticks his head out, letting out a wolf howl.

My cold feet carry me back inside. I close the door with a soft click and press my forehead against the wood, inhaling a trembling breath. Who was she? I haven't seen Grayson bring any women home since his wife's disappearance. If he's had affairs, he's kept them on the down low, away from Chloe.

But she's gone now.

I hurry upstairs to my bedroom and come to a sudden halt in front of my window.

His curtains are drawn.

As I move away, the backs of my legs connect with the bed. Unable to take a full breath, I plop down, my fingers twisting the bedsheet. Is he with her right now?

More to the point, is he fucking her?

Shooting to my feet, I pace, chewing my thumbnail. Why am I so agitated? Why do I have this sudden urge to knock on his door, if only to disturb their cozy little date?

I stop pacing, instead choosing to stare through the window, then start back up. My feet burn a hole in the carpet. Back and forth, from my door to my window, then to my door again.

Is she moaning his name? Does he like it? Does he enjoy how she feels? Is he thinking of me? *Of course,* he's not fucking thinking of me.

Sliding my fingers into my hair, I fist the strands tightly until my scalp prickles. *Stop it, Willow! He's Chloe's father. You have no right to be jealous.*

But I am jealous. I'm so jealous, I want to throw something. I've cooked him countless meals and engaged him in conversation when he was at his lowest. It's thanks to me that he returned to work the other week. If I hadn't encouraged him, he'd be drinking himself to death with his curtains drawn.

Now the curtains are drawn for an entirely different reason.

I resume pacing, chewing my nail to the wick.

CHAPTER 9
WILLOW
FEBRUARY 5TH, 2016

I HATE everything about school these days: the classes, the teachers, the students. Even the ugly brick walls, which have been painted yellow to spruce them up. It's not like it's Easter all year round. I'm struggling to see the point without Chloe. Mom doesn't care, and now that my best friend—my only friend—is gone, my grades are slipping. They resemble a landslide. It's why I'm here with the student counselor in her tiny office with too many fake plants and framed certificates. She's watching me from across the mahogany desk with concerned eyes.

"How are you holding up, Willow?" she asks, adjusting her black-rimmed glasses.

My throat is clogged, but not with emotion—this is something different.

When I don't reply, she offers me a sympathetic smile, then leans forward to open her folder. "Your teachers are worried about you. That's why I called you in here. We know it's been a challenging time for you, losing your best friend." Her eyes flick up to mine and she removes her glasses, placing them down on the desk. "It's only natural that it reflects on your grades, but you're not even trying, Willow."

The clock ticks on the wall. I just want to walk out and never look back.

"How's your mom?"

"She's fine," I reply automatically because it's what I've been hardwired to do. Don't let strangers see the cracks in your facade.

"Have you talked to your mom about community college?"

"My mom is a perfectionist. Nothing less than Harvard would make her proud of me."

Silence.

With a sigh, Mrs. Archer leans back in her creaky desk chair and observes me. "There's nothing wrong with community college."

When I don't respond, she tries a different tactic. "How do you feel about the upcoming vigil?"

Grayson put it off for a long time, holding out hope for his daughter's safe return. Without a body, he's opted for a candle-lit vigil instead of a funeral. It makes sense. No one wants to bury an empty casket.

My chest rises and deflates as I draw in a deep breath. "Like you said, how I feel reflects on my grades."

Her eyes soften and she tucks her curly, blonde hair behind her ear. "You're not alone, Willow."

"That's the thing," my eyes clash with hers, "I *am* alone!"

The sympathy in Mrs. Archer's eyes brings a lump to my throat. I try to swallow past it but fail. "She's gone." My voice breaks. "Chloe is not coming back! And I'm supposed to do what? Care about my grades? Make an effort at school?"

Mrs. Archer says nothing; she just watches me with that look in her eyes. My skin crawls. I don't want her to see what's behind my mask.

I stand up so fast, my chair topples over. "Can I go?"

The clock ticks loudly, crawling beneath my skin. Sighing, she closes my file. "You're free to go."

I don't wait around.

As I walk into the hallway, I collide with a hard chest. Two big hands grip my shoulders to steady me.

"Are you okay?"

I look up, my eyes colliding with Luca's brown irises. We haven't spoken since that night. I avoid him, and I suppose he avoids me too. Neither of us wants to face our guilt for leaving the party together. I lost my best friend, and he lost Dylan. In a sense, we're both to blame for what happened.

"I'm fine." I try to sidestep him, but his hand flies out, grabbing my arm.

He swallows thickly and clears his throat. "Can we talk?"

When I don't respond, he adds, "I brought my car. We can go somewhere."

A group of students shoulders past me, causing me to stumble into Luca again. His hands are back, steadying me.

"Okay," I agree.

When we reach his car, he holds the door open for me. "It's not much, just a rusty little Toyota, but it runs."

"At least you have a car." I get in, and he shuts my door, then rounds the vehicle. The drive to my house is quiet. I suggested we go back to mine since I live closer to school, and Luca's mom works from home.

"It's a big house," Luca comments as he parks in my driveway. I peer out of the windscreen at the white, colonial-style house with gray shutters and a red door.

Instead of replying, I exit the car. Luca, dressed in a black beanie and a thin jacket, follows close behind with his hands shoved deep in his pockets.

Shielded beneath the large entryway from the bright winter sun, I dig in my bag for my keys. Luca is a steady presence at my back, patiently waiting for me to unlock the door so we can exit the cold. My eyes trail over to Grayson's front yard. His car is gone; he must be out. I haven't seen him for a couple of days. It makes me antsy. I keep debating if I should show up with a bag of groceries and offer to cook for him again, but then I remember the woman with the amber hair, and the thought flees my mind as quickly as it entered.

We step into the spacious hallway, and Luca walks ahead while I toe off my shoes and toss my keys in the glass bowl on the console table. It's strange to have him here in my house, scanning his eyes over the framed landscape paintings on the walls. "Let's go to my room."

Sliding past him, I show him the way upstairs. He says nothing, but I sense him close on my heels. I'm not sure why he's here or what he wants to talk about, but I'll hear him out.

As we step into my room, I drop my bag by the door. I avoid looking at him while he inspects the strewn books on my desk before walking the length of my room. "I didn't expect your room to be so… girly."

Mom decorated it. Pink walls and a flowery bedspread topped with enough throw pillows to open a store are not what I would've chosen for myself. I offer him a noncommittal shrug.

He picks up the book on my bedside table, and I fight the heat creeping into my cheeks at seeing him so close to my bed. I've never had a boy in here before, and Luca—dressed in destroyed jeans and a red T-shirt beneath his black jacket—looks out of place next to the pinks and whites.

"It's my current read."

He puts it back down and fingers the gold necklace that hangs from my bedside lamp.

"It was my grandma's," I explain, unsure why I feel like I need to fill the silence with small talk.

Luca scans his eyes over my room once more before sitting down on my bed. I inch closer, wondering if he expects me to join him or if I can stand up while we have this conversation.

"I've been to visit Dylan," he says after a while when the silence becomes too much. "He's not doing so well."

My feet eat up the distance between us, and I carefully lower myself down beside him. I don't speak.

"He, uh, he's gonna plead not guilty."

My eyes fall closed and I release a shaky breath, fisting the comforter to steady myself.

"He seems so fucking sincere. I don't know what to believe."

"Luca..." I whisper, opening my eyes. Grayson's curtains are open, and his bedroom is empty.

The branches sway on the tree between our houses as Luca whispers, "What if he didn't do it? What if the killer is still out there?"

"Her blood was discovered in his bedroom," I reply.

"It was such a small fucking amount. Why would he swear to me that he didn't kill her if he did? It seems so fucking cruel."

I tentatively meet his gaze. It's hard to look at him when his eyes are so intense, full of grief and regret.

"Do you think he did it?" he asks me, and I swallow thickly. I've been dreading the question from the moment he set foot in my house. There's no straightforward answer.

"It doesn't matter what I think," I reply, swiping at my wet cheeks. "He was the last one seen with Chloe; her blood was in his bedroom."

Luca nods slowly, his jaw clenching before he looks away and rests his elbows on his knees. Dragging his fingers though his hair, he blows out a tired breath. "He was my best friend. We've known each other since we were five, or at least I thought we did. This has me questioning everything I thought I knew about him. Because if he's lying to me... If he really did kill her..." His eyes find mine and he looks at me for a long moment. "They've offered him a plea deal."

My breath catches. "They have?"

"A life sentence in turn for a guilty plea."

"But you said..."

"He's gonna plead not guilty, yes."

My hand flies up to my mouth. "The prosecution will pursue the death penalty."

Grinding his teeth, he looks away, staring unseeingly at my window. "It's all my fucking fault! You said you wanted to stay, but I convinced you to leave."

"You can't blame yourself, Luca." I'm a hypocrite. I lie awake at night, wracked with guilt, too.

"I *do* blame myself because it *is* my fault. They'll sentence him to death because of me."

"He killed her, Luca! He sentenced himself to death."

"He swears he's innocent!"

"Do you hear yourself? Don't you think I've asked myself the same questions? It's futile. The evidence says otherwise, Luca. He killed her."

"He's innocent!"

"CHLOE'S BLOOD WAS IN HIS ROOM!" I scream, surprising us both with the sheer power of emotion in my voice. We're glaring at each other, chests panting. Neither of us wants to back down.

In one swift motion, he grabs the back of my head and slams his lips to mine, making me gasp into his mouth. He takes the opportunity to brush his soft tongue against mine; it's the only gentle thing about him. His touch is rough, suffused with anger and guilt. The grief I taste on his hungry lips draws a moan from my throat. I clutch him tighter before shoving his jacket off his shoulders when he guides me onto my back. Climbing on top of me, he shrugs it off, tossing it to the floor, then pulls the back of his T-shirt over his head and discards it too. My hands instinctively find his warm chest, exploring the hard muscles as his lips descend on mine, kissing me until all thoughts leave my head. We're using each other to dull the ache, our shared grief and guilt. If not for us and the decisions we made, we wouldn't be here today.

"Fuck, Willow," Luca moans, gripping my chin and

turning my face to trail a path of scorching kisses down my arched neck.

My eyes collide with Grayson, who stands at his window with his hands in the pockets of his suit pants. His tie is loose, and his sleeves have been rolled up to the elbow. He watches me steadily while Luca slides his hand underneath my tank top and bra cup. Deft fingers tweak my nipples, drawing another soft gasp from my lips. I can't look away from Grayson, not even when Luca dives down to suck on the hardened peak. His warm mouth envelops me, and I let go of him to fist the sheets. I've never felt pleasure like this before. It makes sense now why Chloe always talked to me about sex with Dylan. I've only done it once before. It happened at a party last year. I was drunk, and the guy didn't last more than five minutes. It would be an understatement to call it a disappointment.

Luca pops back up again and grips my chin, forcing my eyes back on his. His mouth descends again, kissing me hungrily while he works his belt buckle.

Breaking away, he shoves his jeans down to his thighs. I roll my head to look at Grayson, but he's gone.

Luca shifts, breathing in my ear as his hand comes to my jeans button. I'm no longer hot. Staring numbly at Grayson's empty room, I wonder what the hell I'm doing. Before I can push Luca off, there's an insistent knock on the front door.

"Don't open it," Luca whispers, popping the button.

I shove him off. "I have to see who it is."

The knocking turns into banging. Luca and I share a look as I straighten my clothes. He pulls his T-shirt back on.

"I'll be right back."

Leaving my room, I hurry down the steps to the entryway. The banging continues before it stops just as abruptly as it started. Grayson peers in through the window, and our eyes lock. I'm strangely relieved. The elation I feel inside me is entirely unwelcome.

When I unlock the door, he slams it open and shoulders past me. "Where the fuck is he?! Is he still in your bedroom?" Grayson doesn't wait around for me to reply as he storms upstairs.

I run after him, pulling on his arm to get him to stop, but he's all muscle and strength. "What the hell are you doing?!"

"I'm throwing the piece of shit out!"

I pause at the top of the stairs, watching him stride down the hallway. Chasing after him, I hiss, "Are you insane?"

He doesn't slow his stride.

Throwing open my bedroom door, he walks straight up to Luca and hauls him up by his T-shirt. "You think you can put your fucking hands on her?"

Luca stutters, "I-I'm sorry, M-Mr. Taylor—"

Grayson drops him. "Mr. Taylor? I'm not her fucking father!"

Luca looks between us before backing out of the room. Without another word, he bolts.

Grayson and I glare at each other in the ensuing silence. Neither one of us speaks until the front door shuts.

"What was that?" I demand. My voice is slightly hysterical. "I can't believe you barged in here and scared him off like that!"

I'm shoved up against the wall, my breath knocked out of me, before I can say another word. With his hand wrapped around my throat, Grayson presses up against me. "You think that *boy*," he spits, "can give you what you need? What you fucking crave?"

"I was more than happy to let him try!" I counter, baring my teeth. Grayson's heady smell surrounds me, intensifying with the glare in his dark eyes. His nostrils flare as he tightens his grip on my throat. Just when I think he's going to snap and devour me, he drops me instead.

Pointing his finger, he warns, "If I see him here again, I'll beat him to a fucking pulp. Don't test me!"

Then he's gone, and I'm left fuming with crescent moons on my palms.

CHAPTER 10
GRAYSON
FEBRUARY 11TH, 2016

I'M SCANNING the crowds for Willow when I feel a hand on my shoulder blade. As I turn around, I'm met with Margaret's sorrow-filled eyes. "What a beautiful vigil, Grayson."

My smile is weak. I've put this off for a long time now because I wasn't ready to accept the truth: my daughter is gone. Skelton is a small town with a tight-knit community, so today's turnout is overwhelming. The sun is out, warming tear-streaked cheeks and offering a glimmer of light on an otherwise dark and gloomy day.

It turns out Margaret was only the beginning. I'm shaking hands and accepting condolences for the next half an hour before the crowd finally starts to thin.

I need to apologize to Willow for what I did the other week, barging in like that and acting like a jealous boyfriend. I had no right. I don't know what the hell it is about her that makes me lose my wits, which is why I've kept my distance. I can't let myself feel these emotions. I'm a middle-aged man. The last thing I need is to entangle myself with a teenage girl.

I look for her one last time, but she's gone. Despite being Chloe's best friend, she kept a low profile at the back during the vigil. Willow prefers to blend in rather than stand out. On a day like this, I wanted to respect that side of her. It's why I never asked her to do a speech.

I find her waiting for me on my porch when I arrive home. I'm surprised, but at the same time, I'm not. Today has been an especially difficult day for us both.

"Can I come in?" she asks as I approach.

My eyes skate down to the bottle of wine in her hand, and I frown. "Where did you get that?"

"Where do you think?" Rising to her feet, she steadies herself on the railing. "Mom's stash."

"I haven't seen your mom in a long while," I comment, unlocking the front door.

"Well, you wouldn't," she says. "She's never home."

I help Willow into the hallway and shut the door behind us. As I walk her into the living room, she swigs her bottle of wine and I snatch it off her, placing it on a high shelf where she can't reach it.

Unfocused fiery, blue eyes find mine. "What the hell, Grayson?!"

"You've had enough!" I grab her arm and drag her over to the couch. Placing my hand on her shoulder, I guide her to sit.

"Why did you drink so much?"

"You, out of everyone, should know."

I lower myself down across from her on the coffee table. "You're not dealing well with Chloe's disappearance."

Her bitter, drunken laughter fills the room as she falls back against the cushions. She pins me with her eyes. "Is grief linear? Is it okay to almost drink yourself to death for a few months, provided you get your shit together after," she makes quotation marks, "'an agreeable amount of time' has passed?"

"I never said that."

"I didn't let myself feel at first. You had too much of your own grief to handle. I wanted to make you smile again, but now… I can't be strong for-fucking-ever."

"You want more alcohol? Is that it? You think it'll numb the fucking pain?" I growl. I should discourage her instead of supplying a minor with alcohol but fuck that. If she wants to hurt for one day, I'll let her.

At least she's safe.

I clap my thighs and stand up to retrieve her wine. There's a twinge of guilt when she drinks it all, but she's weeks away from being a legal adult. She's not a child.

"You feel better?" I ask.

She blinks at me with her glassy eyes. "No…"

I knew she wouldn't. Alcohol doesn't take the problems away. It dulls the pain, sure, but you can't outrun grief. Once it's touched you, it's a companion for life.

"Who was that woman?"

My brows pull down low. Willow sees my confusion and adds, "The woman with amber hair."

Realization dawns. "She was no one."

Instead of being reassured, a mask falls over her face. "Are you seeing her again?"

It was a random fuck. I talked to her online for a few days, and we agreed to meet. I needed to release some of this pent-up energy that seems to gain momentum when I spend time with Willow.

"No, I'm not seeing her again."

"Why?" she asks, spreading her legs slightly. My eyes fall to her smooth thighs. Her skirt has ridden up, revealing a glimpse of white lace.

"I haven't spoken to her since then."

"Why?"

I swallow thickly when she spreads her thighs wider. There's no doubt about it—she's trying to seduce me. "She hasn't messaged me."

She slowly trails her fingers up her thighs, closer to her center. "But if she did, would you meet up with her?"

My throat jumps and I shake my head to try to clear it. "It was a one-time thing."

She hums, placing her heels on the edge of the couch.

I should stop this.

But I don't.

"You must have been a bad lay."

Frowning, my eyes skate up to hers. "What?"

"You fucked her, but she didn't message you after." Her fingers disappear beneath the lace fabric.

Holy shit. My eyes fly back down, and I swallow thickly.

"You must not know how to please a woman."

I fight down a groan when she arches her back and lets out a loud moan. I'm trapped in her web, knowing I should walk out, but I can't. Her words slowly sink in, denting my ego.

In the next second, I'm on my knees before her, spreading her thighs wide and sliding her lace panties aside. Her soaking, pink little cunt glistens, making me groan. "You think I don't know how to please a woman?"

She tugs sharply on my hair, forcing me closer to her swollen pussy lips. "I think Luca would have done a better job."

That does it. Gripping her hips, I cover her pussy with my mouth, sucking her clit between my lips. She tastes fucking divine, like innocence mixed with devilish intent. She cries out, causing my dick to throb in its denim confines.

"You think Luca could make you feel this good?" I taunt, then flatten my tongue and drag it over her pussy, from her anus to clit. Before she can respond, I fill her up with my finger and pay homage to her swollen clit. I lick it in fast circles while pumping my finger. Arousal seeps out of her, and I lick up every drop, growling against her throbbing pussy. "You taste so fucking amazing!"

"Grayson," she whimpers, rolling her hips. "God, Grayson, please."

Smirking, I blow on her clit. "You soon ate your words, huh, sweetheart." Inserting a second finger, I spread her cunt while I suck on each pussy lip in turn. "So fucking beautiful."

She's shaking, shivering, her toes curling, and her eyes roll to the back of her head. I keep going, licking her pussy like it's my personal mission to ruin her for other men. "You think teenage boys can lick you this good?" I force a third finger inside her, pumping her tight cunt. "Finger fuck you this good? No, sweetheart, only Daddy can."

She releases a keening sound that makes me chuckle against her soaking cunt. With her daddy issues, I knew she would have a daddy kink. I felt her clench just now. She loved it. Shifting up, I grab the back of the couch while I continue thrusting my fingers inside her tight heat. My lips brush her ear and I smirk slowly, sensing her shiver. "One day, you'll let Daddy fuck this sweet cunt, won't you, Willow?"

I stare directly into her eyes as I flick her clit with my thumb. "Look down." When her gaze lowers and her pussy squeezes my fingers, I whisper, "You're Daddy's good little slut, aren't you? Look at you, taking three fingers."

"Oh god," she moans again, biting her plump bottom lip. I remove my hand from her heat and pull her lip away from her teeth before forcing my fingers inside her mouth. "That's it, sweetheart, show me how well you suck cock. Give me something to imagine tonight when I fuck my hand."

Her pretty mouth eagerly sucks me down, but it's not enough. The darkness in me, the hurt and the anger, wants more. Straddling her on the couch, I fist her hair and force my fingers down her throat, whispering, "Relax, sweetheart."

Tears spring to her eyes and seep out, and I drink up the sight like an addict with his drug of choice. My dick has never been harder than it is right now at the sight of her submissive, teary eyes goading me on.

"Fuck!" I growl, barely able to restrain myself. Fucking her would cross a line I can't cross. Getting her off is one thing, but using my daughter's best friend for my own needs?

Sliding my fingers back out and shifting onto the floor, I cover her pussy with my mouth again. My dick throbs so badly, it's painful. I need release. I need it so fucking bad. Gripping her hip tightly, I use my free hand to unbuckle my jeans and slide the zipper down. With the sight of her creamy thighs spread wide and her pink, glistening pussy—her tight hole stretched open from my fingers—I'm about to combust. Latching onto her clit, I shove my jeans down and palm my cock, sliding my hand over the thick, throbbing length.

"Grayson," she moans, pulling sharply on my hair. "Please, I want you."

Leaning back on my knees, I make sure she can see me touching myself. "You want this, sweetheart? You want Daddy's cock?"

"Please," she moans again, squeezing her tits through the thin fabric of her tank top. "I need you."

I stroke my dick faster. "Show me your breasts."

She's obedient, following orders like a good little slut.

Damn, those rosy, hard nipples. As I continue stroking myself, she tweaks them. "Touch yourself. Let me see you fuck your pretty cunt."

Her eyes hold mine while her hand trails down her stomach, dipping between her legs. Precum beads on my dick and spills over when her lips part as she starts to rub her clit. "Feels good, doesn't it, Willow?"

"Yes, Daddy."

Shit. I never thought I was into that, but the way it slips off her swollen, moist lips… I nearly fucking come.

"Are you close?"

"So close!" she breathes out.

"Keep your eyes open." I climb to my feet and brace my knees against the couch, staring down at her as I stroke my big cock over her lithe body. Because I can't help myself, I reach out to squeeze her breasts. They're a perfect handful, molding to my hand like they were fucking made for me. I pinch her nipple until she whimpers in pain. "That's it, sweetheart. Keep fucking yourself."

Her blue eyes, half-mast and heavy with lust, stare up at me. I'm so fucking close.

Cupping her chin, I tip her face up, ordering, "Come for me. Now."

She's so damn responsive. When I press down on her lips with my thumb, her body tenses up, and her mouth parts on a silent scream.

"Fuck," I growl, letting go of my control. My fingers dig into her chin as jets of cum shower over her chest and belly.

When I've milked my dick dry, I zip myself away and drag my fingers through the cum on her chest. As I bring them up to her lips, she surprises me by seizing my wrist and snatching my digits up with her hot, hungry mouth. She sucks them clean, then whispers, "More, Daddy."

I trail my fingers through it again and drag them over her tongue as she sticks it out and flattens it like a good girl. Then I do it again and again until my little whore is satisfied.

"Good girl," I praise, grabbing her chin and forcing her gaze up to mine. "If you ever let another man see you like this, Willow…"

Releasing her, I let my threat hang in the air between us as I walk out.

With any luck, she won't remember this tomorrow, and I can go back to pretending I'm a good guy. I said I shouldn't cross the line. Well, I just did.

CHAPTER 11
WILLOW
FEBRUARY 12TH, 2016

"MOM?" I call out, wincing as I descend the carpeted stairs. My head hurts after the copious amount of alcohol I consumed last night.

Nothing but silence greets me. It snowed in the night, and the house is cold. An inch of snow covers the window. Stepping into the kitchen, I gaze at the flurries outside before rubbing my arms to ward off the chill. There's a note on the kitchen island.

There's a pasta dish in the fridge.
Mom.

I leave it where it is and walk back out. The floorboards creak beneath my feet as I make my way down the hallway to the living room. I should get ready for school, but I don't. Instead, I snuggle up beneath a blanket on the couch and stare at the snowflakes through the patio doors. The lawn is white, peppered with animal footprints that lead into the forest where our yard ends. The trees, with their spindly branches, are covered in a dusting of snow. I love this time of the year, even if I don't enjoy the cold. There's a peacefulness about winter that can't be found in summer—a silence. Not the oppressive kind that lives in my house. This is gentle, a whisper on the breeze, urging me closer.

I'm just about to drift off to sleep when there's a knock on the door. I startle awake, and when it comes again, I throw off my quilt. With my arms wrapped around myself, I enter the hallway, wishing I had put on my bathrobe. It's too cold for sleep shorts and a T-shirt.

I'm met with a cold breeze as I unlock the door and inch it open.

Grayson smiles at me. "How are you feeling this morning?"

"Like I've had too much to drink," I reply honestly. My mouth tasted like a brewery when I woke up. I brushed my teeth three times, and it still wasn't enough.

Grayson, dressed in jeans and a black, wooly jumper beneath his jacket, watches me like he's waiting for something before his lips spread in a disarming smile. "Are you going to let me in?"

The door creaks as I open it all the way. Flurries of snow drift over the threshold on a gentle breeze, melting on the tips of my toes. I shiver and step aside for Grayson, who shrugs out of his jacket. My cheeks heat at the memory of what we did the previous night. I'd had a lot to drink, but not too much to recall what happened. My pussy is sore from his ministrations.

Deliciously sore.

"It's cold in here. Want me to start a fire?" He walks ahead, entering the living room at the end of the hallway. When I catch up, he's crouched before the mantelpiece, stacking wood in the fireplace.

With his back to me, he says, "I didn't see any footprints in the snow, so I figured you were skipping school today."

I take a seat on the couch and wrap the blanket around myself. "I didn't have it in me to face everyone today."

His shoulders move as he reaches for the matchsticks. When the fire is lit, he looks at me behind him. "Want to talk about it?"

"No," I reply honestly, shaking my head. "If anything, I want to forget. I want to pretend everything is normal."

Rising to his feet, he walks up to me and tips my chin with his finger. His thumb brushes over my mouth as he searches my eyes. I can't read him. "What do you remember of last night?"

My tingling lips part and my tongue darts out to taste him, stealing his attention. "Grayson," I whisper, sucking his thumb into my mouth and reaching out to squeeze the outline of his hard cock. His hips jerk forward, and he grips my chin hard, forcing my head back until his dark eyes pin me to the spot. "Take me out."

Just as I reach for his belt, the front door opens.

"Mom?"

Grayson stiffens and steps back, quickly adjusting his dick in his pants.

I look over my shoulder when my brother, Liam, steps into the room with a backpack on his shoulder. He looks from me to Grayson. "Hi?" There's a question in his tone before he trains his eyes on me. "Shouldn't you be at school?"

My brother's dirty-blonde hair is shorter than the last time I saw him, and the tips glisten with melting snowflakes. Sliding his bag off his shoulder, he sets it down on the floor, then straightens up.

"I should get going," Grayson says. "The fire is set up for you, Willow. If you need anything else, just knock."

He walks out without another backward glance, and I curse my brother for his stupid timing.

"Is that the next-door neighbor?"

Liam is seven years older than me. As a result, he doesn't know Chloe's family like I do.

"Why are you back?"

My brother shrugs. "I have time off work, and I haven't been home for a while. With everything that's going on, I thought—"

"You thought what?" I ask, standing up. It's so typical of him to show up now. He's ignored us for the last eighteen months and didn't even remember to call on Mom's birthday, but now he shows up? Several months *after* Chloe's disappearance?

"I don't buy it, Liam. You're after money." I walk past him into the kitchen, where I proceed to make a sandwich.

He saunters in after me, gazing around as if he's never seen this room before, despite growing up here. His eyes land on the note on the kitchen island. Picking it up, he reads Mom's scrawled handwriting, then tosses it back down and opens the fridge.

The butter is too hard, and my bread starts to fall apart. I'm tempted to give up and just have cereal.

"Where's the pasta?"

I roll my eyes and shoulder him out of the way to grab the cheese. "I ate it. You're a day too late for leftovers. That note is from last night."

He watches me cut the cheese and pop a slice into my mouth.

"What?" I ask him when he continues staring.

"Nothing. You've grown, that's all."

"I would hope so," I reply, placing the cheese slices on my sandwich and putting the cheese and butter back inside the fridge. "It's been a year and a half since I last saw you."

"How is mom's new job going?"

I shut the fridge door. "She started it shortly before you left, remember? If you called home once in a while, you'd know she left because of the shift patterns. Speaking of jobs, how is yours going?"

My brother lives in a large city across the country, where he works as a mechanic. Why he couldn't do that here in Skelton is anyone's guess, but Liam had always dreamed of moving away.

"What was the neighbor doing here?" he asks, changing the subject.

I finish chewing before replying. "I ran out of firewood. Grayson offered to help me light the fire."

"It's his daughter, isn't it, who disap…"

I nod.

"The boyfriend did it?"

My sandwich tastes like ash. I swallow down the piece in my mouth before throwing the rest in the garbage and walking back out of the kitchen. Liam is hot on my heels.

I whirl around at the bottom of the steps. "How long are you here for this time before disappearing again?"

"I—"

"Because it hurts Mom when you come home to visit and then vanish again for months without a word." I don't tell him that it hurts to be second best. Liam was always the favorite child. Mom never ignored him, but she still blames me. Somehow, it's my fault he left home.

Drawing in a sigh, he rubs the back of his neck. "I'm a shit son, okay? I know that."

Snorting, I set off up the stairs. "Welcome home, brother."

CHAPTER 12
WILLOW
FEBRUARY 15TH, 2016

WHEN I SHUT MY LOCKER, I come face to face with Luca. "Jesus, I nearly jumped out of my skin!"

He's ditched his beanie for a red, backward cap and a black puffer vest. Dressed in a camouflage T-shirt underneath, the muscles in his bare arms are on full display. "Who was that the other day?"

I frown, leaning my shoulder against my locker. "What are you talking about, Luca?"

The hallway bustles with students on their way to class, and it forces Luca closer to me when a girl asks to open the locker he's leaning on.

"You know when we… The old guy who threw me out."

"The old guy?" I release a soft laugh.

"Was that Chloe's dad?"

I wet my lips, scanning the hallway for listening ears. "Yes, Chloe and I were neighbors, remember?"

"He seemed possessive."

Done with this conversation, I push off the locker and start walking. Luca chases after me. Figuring it's best to offer him an explanation, a reason not to dig deeper, I reply, "Chloe and

I grew up close. Grayson is as much a father to me as he was to Chloe."

"That's it, sweetheart. Show me how well you suck cock. Give me something to imagine tonight when I fuck my hand."

"That explains it, I suppose. He behaved like—"

Whirling on him, I bark, "Like what, Luca? What did he behave like?"

He looks confused, brows pulled low, mouth pursed. "Like your boyfriend."

"Eww, gross! He's Chloe's dad." I walk off again. This is bad, bad, bad. The last thing I need is for Luca to be suspicious.

"Hey, where are you running off to?" he asks, catching up.

"Class, Luca."

"Can we go somewhere?"

Blowing out a sigh, I pause outside the classroom. "Why? I'm not making out with you again."

"I get that!" he almost growls, stepping close before inhaling shakily. "That's not what this is about."

Students file past us, entering the classroom. I wait for them to pass.

"There's no one I can talk to. What happened, it's…"

I get it. Our mutual guilt is a lonely place. No one else here can share it with us. It was him and me that night, driving away from our friends.

"The trial starts in six weeks," he continues, reaching for my hand and interlacing his fingers with mine. The world fades out, blurring into the background as his warm hand squeezes mine. I can almost taste his pain on my tongue as it pulsates in the crackling air between us. I'm barely aware of the students streaming past us when he pulls me closer. "I'm a mess, Willow."

❄

"FUCK, FUCK, FUCK!" he grunts, pistoning his hips against me. It's cramped in the backseat of his Toyota, and my head smashes against the passenger door with every thrust. His fingers dig into my hips as he groans against my neck, his big cock pulsing inside me.

He's sweaty and spent. I'm empty and hollow.

Crawling off me, he sits upright and lifts his ass off the seat to pull up his jeans. His buckle clinks while he fastens it.

I sit up too, then slide my skirt back down. I take off my ruined panties, using them to wipe away the cum that's seeping out of me.

Removing his cap, Luca slides a hand over his hair before placing it back on. Then he looks at me. "What the fuck are we doing?"

His cum keeps leaking out of me. I toss my soaked panties down in the footwell. "You tell me, Luca."

"Hell if I know. I just want the fucking pain gone."

There's a thick lump clogged in my throat, and when I look at Luca, his Adam's apple jumps. He shares my pain. I've never had that before, someone who understands me, and I don't know how to handle it.

"This was a mistake."

"Yeah, it was," he agrees, shifting on the seat. He grabs my ankles and pulls me down, crawling over me. His fingers slide over my swollen pussy, and he shoves a digit inside my tight heat. I'm sore from when he entered me earlier before I was sufficiently wet. I don't care. I just want to forget. If Luca wants to hurt me to dull his own pain, I'll spread my legs like a whore in the back of his car.

"I keep thinking," I whisper while he continues fingering me, "how do we ever move on? My grades are failing. I'm supposed to go to college, but I can't make myself care about any of it. I just want to disappear."

"We're a mess," he replies, leaning down to suck my

bottom lip between his teeth. "Fuck, your pussy is tight. Do you like it when I finger you?"

"I like how my body responds." My hips lift off the damp leather, chasing his touch, rolling in time with his pumps. "I don't like how I feel on the inside, the suffocating darkness…"

His response is a second finger as he whispers, "Come with me to the trial. I need you there."

"But Grayso—"

"Fuck Grayson!" Unbuckling his belt, he flips me over onto my front and yanks my skirt up to my waist. "It's you and me." He enters me from behind, slamming his hips home hard and pulling on my hair as if it soothes him to punish me for letting him talk me into leaving that night. "No one else gets it, Willow. They didn't see them fight. Grayson didn't do wrong by his daughter. But you and I, we abandoned our best friends." His warm breath heats my damp neck. "I could fuck you all day long. You have no fucking idea how good you feel."

I squeeze my eyes shut as he takes me harder, the fabric of his puffer vest rustling behind me. There's nothing sweet or gentle about this union. We're not in love. We barely even like each other. This is two lost souls soaking up each other's pain. Fucking like rabbits in his steamed-up Toyota to the soundtrack of slapping skin and moans.

I let myself be carried away in his current, my pussy squeezing around his throbbing dick. I don't want to be good and make the right decisions. I want to self-destruct and externalize this inner pain, this darkness that has its claws in me.

CHAPTER 13
WILLOW

"THAT'S JUST WEIRD, SIS!" my brother says, stopping in the doorway to the kitchen. "What the fuck are you doing?"

I don't lift my forehead off the kitchen island. "I'm cursing myself for making bad life decisions. Ever done that? Made shit decisions that'll come back to bite you later in life?"

Liam steps over the threshold as I finally straighten up. "I make shit decisions all the time, but I don't bang my head on the island for five minutes straight."

"Shut up," I grumble, rubbing my sore forehead. "It wasn't five minutes."

Liam rips down the note attached to the fridge with a magnet. "Mom's out again."

"Where is she this time?" I scoot my chair back and walk over to him, snatching the note from his fingers. "Gone for a meal with Sarah and Jane," I read out loud. "Well, there's a surprise."

"She's never home, huh?"

When I don't reply, he turns me around with his hands on my shoulders. "How about we go to the movies? I'll let you pick what to watch."

I toss the note on the counter and shrug. "Sure." It's not like I'm doing anything else tonight.

We take a taxi there, and Liam fills the ride with small talk. He's always been outgoing and quick to laugh. It's easy to see how he ended up living in a large city while I'm stuck here in Skelton, with the tractors and toothpick-chewing farmers.

Liam pays for the taxi and the movie tickets. I try to pay for the popcorn and drinks, but he waves me off. "It's my treat."

I'm not sure how to feel about his attention. It's obvious he feels sympathy for me—his little sister who is always alone in our mom's big house. I wish he would stay, even if he annoys me more often than not. His absence echoes louder than his stomping feet on the stairs or his incessant talking.

We settle in our seats toward the back, and I take a moment to pretend that this is my life—that I'm a girl with a family who loves her. My heart clenches behind its prison bars. The sad truth is that this is my first time at the movies with anyone else besides Chloe.

While the film plays, Liam stuffs his mouth with popcorn as though he's performing a magic trick to impress onlookers with how much he can fit in there. It's impossible not to gawk. My eyes soon snag on something else—or rather, *someone* else.

Two rows ahead, at the end of the aisle, is a broad set of shoulders I'm all too familiar with.

Grayson.

And he's not alone. The girl with amber hair is back, leaning with her head on his shoulder.

Something ugly grows inside me, but I'm torn from my inner anguish when Liam nudges my shoulder.

"This is the best part."

My brows knit together. "I thought you hadn't seen this movie before."

Leaning close, he flashes a smile. "I lied."

Clearly.

My eyes land on Grayson again while the movie music rises to a crescendo as the car chase on screen ends in a large explosion. I'm up on my feet, squeezing past legs in my hurry to get out. I make sure to walk past the row where he sits, and when I pass him, I tap his shoulder. I don't have to wait long outside for him to join me. Blinking against the lights, he looks far too delicious in a denim shirt with a white T-shirt underneath and black jeans. "Willow, what's wrong?"

His question pisses me off, and I shove him firmly before walking off. His thunderous footsteps catch up with me and he drags me into the family bathroom, then flips the lock.

"The hell is your problem?!"

"You're with her?" I shout, irate, vaguely aware of the cramped room that stinks of piss and cheap, citrusy air freshener.

"What's it to you?"

I repeat his words from the afternoon after the vigil. "If you ever let another man see you like this, Willow…"

Dragging his big hand down his face, Grayson chuckles, but the masculine sound is void of humor. "It was a mistake. I shouldn't have touched you."

His words hurt, slicing me like a sharp knife. Rejection is a flavor I've tasted before, yet my tastebuds never adjust. It's as foul every time.

"You know that 'boy' Luca?" I whisper, stepping close enough to breathe in his smell: cologne and soap. "I let him fuck me in the backseat of his Toyota today."

His hand flies out and wraps around my throat, forcing me up onto my tiptoes. "Careful, Willow. I'm not in control around you."

"Is that why you fuck her? Because you're in control?"

Baring his teeth, he tightens his grip on me, stealing my breath. "I fuck her because she's a good lay." With a cruel smile, he adds, "An *experienced* lay. She knows what she's doing, unlike little girls like you."

Now it's my turn to mask my hurt with a smirk. "You like loose pussy, Grayson? Is that it?"

He cuts off my airflow again. I fucking love how he lets his snarling monster out from the shadows when I coax it out to play. "You're jealous, sweetheart. You're jealous because I'll take her home and fuck her brains out after the movie while you sit on your bed, staring at my drawn curtains." Leaning in close, he whispers in my ear, "I might leave them open tonight. Let you watch me ravage her."

"I won't be home," I choke out. "I'll be on all fours in Luca's bed."

Spinning us around, he shoves me up against the door and snakes his hand inside my skirt. His fingers hook the fabric of my panties and slide them aside while he breathes in my ear, his lips spreading in a dark smile against my sensitive skin. He shoves two fingers into me and clamps his hand over my mouth to silence my pained whimper. I'm sore after Luca.

"Give Daddy your pain, sweetheart," he growls, pumping me hard and deep. "Let me see those tears trailing down your cheeks."

When I spread my thighs wider, he chuckles. "You think I'll be gentle with you when you let that boy have what's mine?" He shoves a third finger inside me, making me cry out beneath his hand. "Your pussy belongs to me."

This dark and toxic part of Grayson is what I've come to crave the most. I want him to hurt me and punish me. While he's knuckle-deep in my sore cunt, feasting on my tears and whimpers, that bitch is watching the movie alone.

"You want more pain, sweetheart?"

I nod eagerly, and he slides his fingers out to undo his jeans. The distinct sound of his belt buckle being undone raises goosebumps on my skin. I'm finally about to feel his big cock stretch my pussy. I've wanted to fuck Grayson since I first started noticing boys. I still remember the afternoon I walked into his living room and found him lifting weights shirtless. I still touch myself to the memory of the thick veins on his arms and his bulging muscles.

"I won't fuck you nice, sweetheart. Not after you spread your legs for that boy. Understood? I'll treat you like my own fuck toy and then leave you here with my cum trickling down your chin."

Lifting me up against the door, he spreads my thighs wide and teases my clit with his finger. "Look how pretty and pink your pussy is." He pinches my throbbing clit. "How soaked you are for me."

He thrusts forward, then immediately pulls out and slams back in, ensuring I don't have time to adjust. It hurts so fucking good. Digging my nails into his shoulders, I cling to him while he pounds me against the door, ignoring the knocking on the outside.

They can wait.

"This pussy…" he grunts, grabbing me by my throat. "There's nothing quite like it. I can't fucking control myself around you."

"Grayson," I moan, and he grips my face, forcing my mouth open by digging his fingers into my cheeks. Then he kisses me hard, devouring me with punishing lashes of his tongue and stinging bites while he holds my face frozen.

"You can fuck that boy all day long," he breathes out, "but you know he can't give you what you crave."

Before I can reply, he cuts off my oxygen with his hand wrapped around my throat and whispers, "You belong to me, Willow. Your smiles are mine, your body is mine, and your pussy is mine. Even your breaths belong to me."

Darkness seeps in at the edges and I begin to struggle. Grayson fucks me harder. "You can breathe again after you've been a good girl and come on my cock." Reaching down, he rubs my clit while his fingers bruise my neck. As my eyes lock with his, every muscle in my body tenses. I fall over the edge as stars explode behind my eyes.

His grip eases up on my throat, and his dick slips out when he sets me down on my feet. I'm weak and shaking.

"That's my girl," he praises, stroking my hair out of my face before cupping my chin. "I'm going to come in your mouth, and you'll swallow every last drop, sweetheart. Understood?"

I nod softly as he applies pressure to my shoulders. My knees connect with the cold, sticky floor and rough hands pull my hair up in a ponytail while I sway, unsteady. Grayson slaps my cheek gently. "Open that pretty mouth."

I can barely keep my eyes open—I'm that exhausted from his brutal fucking. But I do as instructed, gagging when his cock hits the back of my throat.

His grip on my hair tightens, his cock twitching in my mouth. "Look at me, Willow. Give me those beautiful eyes."

My gaze slides up, locking on his, and he thrusts his hips. When I choke, he holds me frozen, my hair twisted in a tight pony. He picks up the pace, fucking my mouth faster with deep rolls of his hips. "Fuck, that's it. Relax. Let Daddy have that tight throat."

I try to breathe through my nose, but it's difficult when he gives me no respite and no time to catch my breath. My nails dig into his thighs. I push back against him, but he takes what he wants.

"Did you let that boy fuck your face?" Pulling out, he slaps my cheek with his dick. "Did you?"

"No."

Forcing his fingers into my mouth, his other hand in my hair, he drags his digits over my tongue before replacing them with his cock.

Two more thrusts... three... four... *"Fuck!"* His hot cum hits the back of my throat and beads on my tongue. Pulling out, he slams my mouth shut and says, "Swallow! Don't let it escape."

When I've followed his instructions, he steps back and tucks his cock away. Then he roughly palms my face before cupping my chin and guiding my eyes up to his. "Act like a whore, and I'll fuck you like one."

His words are meant to humiliate. If Daddy wants to play, I'll set out the pieces on the board. Spreading my knees on the sticky floor, I fall forward on my hands. Gazing up at him from beneath my dark lashes, I purr, "What makes Daddy think I want to be fucked like a good girl?"

I don't miss the clenching of his fists. He's trying to control himself.

I don't like control.

"Come out to play, Daddy," I purr, rocking on the floor and jutting my ass out. "Hurt me, Daddy, claim me. Fuck me like a slut."

His queen topples over, and he escapes the room as though he's on fire.

Sitting back on my ass, I smile to myself. Grayson is mine. We both know the woman with amber hair can't give him what he wants. She's afraid of his monster that lurks in the shadows. She doesn't set traps to lure it out like I do. Unlike me, she shies away from the darkness in his gaze.

CHAPTER 14
GRAYSON
FEBRUARY 22ND, 2016

I FEEL LIKE A FUCKING PERVERT, waiting in my car for Willow to finish school. If anyone asks, I'm here to take her home.

Since the time I fucked her in the bathroom at the movies, I haven't stopped thinking about her. It's like she crawled beneath my skin and dug her claws into me.

I need more of her drug. I need to bury myself balls deep in her sweet pussy and forget about the world and the upcoming trial. Who the fuck cares that she's three weeks away from her eighteenth birthday? I've already crossed the line.

And the monster inside me is growing restless, pacing in its cage.

It's time to let him out.

She jogs down the steps, and I wait for her to notice my car. She doesn't disappoint. She comes to a halt, staring directly at me behind the steering wheel. Her small side-smirk makes my dick twitch in my jeans.

Walking up to the car, she gets in and says with a teasing lilt in her voice, "Looking for trouble, Mr. Reid?"

"The worst kind of trouble." I turn the key in the ignition.

The roads are busy at this time of the day, full of parents collecting their kids from school. We've barely reached the main road when I loosen my tie before placing my hand on her bare thigh and inching up her skirt. Her legs spread for me, granting me better access.

Glancing down, I groan when I catch sight of the damp patch on her red, lacy panties. "You wet for me already, sweetheart? I haven't touched you yet."

My pinkie brushes up against her mound, and she gasps audibly.

It makes me smile.

"I haven't seen you in a week, Grayson. Now you're here, treating me like a queen. What changed?"

"I can't stay away any longer." I inch her panties aside when we slow at a stoplight. The man in the car next to us has his eyes trained forward, none the wiser to my wandering fingers.

"Fuck," I growl, peering down at her soaking pussy. "Your cunt is so damn pretty. Let me see you finger yourself."

"You're very demanding today, Daddy," she teases, spreading her pussy lips with her fingers. "You like what you see?"

"Damn straight, I do."

Two of her fingers disappear into her wet heat before sliding back out, glistening with her arousal. I groan out loud. Fuck, she drives me insane.

"I wish it was your fingers."

"It will be soon. Keep fingering yourself. Let me hear you moan for me."

I step on the gas while she spreads her thighs wider, thrusting deeper. She's so damn beautiful, it's hard to look away.

"Good girl! You turn me on so fucking much."

"Grayson," she moans, arching her neck as her creamy thighs begin to quiver. "I need you inside me."

I rip open the glovebox. "Fuck yourself with that."

Straightening up, she removes the lifelike dildo I bought her. It's not as big as my cock, but it's a decent size to get her ready for me. I'm salivating at the thought of seeing her pussy stretch around it.

Because she's a tease who likes to watch me squirm, she wraps her lips around the big head and sucks it deeper while she moans.

My teeth sink into my bottom lip, and I grip the steering wheel so hard, my knuckles turn white.

She removes it with a pop and slowly trails it down her body. By the time it sinks inside her, I'm fucking panting through my nose.

"That's it, sweetheart. Take it deep."

"Oh, fuck," she moans.

I love that she has no reservations about who might see her. If anything, judging by how wet she is, she's turned on by the idea of a driver in a different car spotting her.

Her feminine, soft whimpers have me leaking precum as I finally pull over at a local lookout spot. I cut the engine, then lean back against the door, allowing myself a moment to watch her fuck herself.

"Show me your tits."

"I can't. I'm so close."

In one swift motion, I shift forward and grab her by the throat. "Show me your damn tits!"

She's not fast enough, so I shove her top down, not caring in the slightest that I tear the fabric in the process. Her tits spill free, creamy and full, with pebbled, rosy nipples. Palming her breast, I lean down to suck one of the buds between my teeth, then the other one.

She yelps when I slap her tit, watching it bounce.

"Fuck," I groan. "They're so damn pert and perfect!" I slap it again, pleased when her pale skin reddens. This time, when

I take her nipple in my mouth, I bite down hard until she cries out.

"You're gonna please me, sweetheart?"

"Yes," she breathes out, arching her tits closer to my smirking lips.

"Get out of the car and lean over the hood with your ass in the air."

Frowning, she moves back, searching my face. "Anyone could spot us."

My hand flies out, grabbing her chin. "Do as I fucking say."

With a soft nod, she reaches behind her and opens the door. The area is away from the main road and shielded by trees, but it's still public land, and anyone could walk by.

I like that thought. I reach onto the backseat for the Halloween mask I brought in case someone spots us. As much as I love her pussy, I would be no good to her in jail.

Putting it on and stepping out, I admire her creamy ass on top of my hood. She watches me over her shoulder as I stalk her.

"What's with the 'Jason' mask?" she asks, staring wide-eyed at me.

"Spread your legs wider. As far as you can."

She obeys.

The insides of her thighs are soaking wet, a trail of pussy juice running down her leg. She's going to be the death of me.

Falling to my knees behind her, I lift my mask and drag my tongue through the trail, all the way up to her pink pussy. My tongue slides through her folds as I grip her ass and spread her apart. With my face soaked in her arousal, I circle the soft curve of her entrance before stretching her with my tongue and feeling her clench around me.

"Grayson," she moans. Her sweet sounds echo through the trees.

I slap her ass hard, relishing in her sharp gasp.

She's fucking divine. How am I going to survive this? How am I ever going to walk away from her? The truth is, I can't. I'm hers completely now. Maybe it's wrong to be this obsessed with someone like her—my daughter's best friend—but I can't stop this obsession from growing.

I want to possess her, own every part of her until she doesn't know where she begins and I end.

I suck on her clit and feast on her until she's shaking beneath my tight grip on her thighs.

Rising to my feet, I pull my mask back down and slap her pussy hard. Then I do it again when she yelps.

"Quiet. You'll take what I give you, sweetheart."

Gripping her neck, I press her cheek against the hood, brushing her hair away from her eyes. "Are you ready for me?"

"Please, Grayson, please."

I swiftly unbuckle my belt and pull down my zipper. My suit pants pool around my ankles as I stroke my hard dick. I can't wait to lose myself in her, to feel her wrapped around me.

Rubbing my cock over her pussy, I coat it in her slickness and then bring the hard tip to her puckered hole. I press forward just enough to feel her stiffen.

I like her fear.

I want more of it.

"Every part of you belongs to me, Willow. I'm going to fuck your ass one day soon."

Before she can respond, I take her pussy, burying myself to the hilt in her heat. I grit my teeth against the intense pleasure. I'll blow my load like a teenage boy if I'm not careful. I can't fucking help it when she's so damn tight, it's almost painful.

Her loud moans are music to my ears as I begin to move, watching my cock enter her greedy pussy over and over again. "That's it, sweetheart. You're doing so fucking well."

I pull out and finger her tight cunt until my fingers are nice and soaked.

"Please, I need your dick," she whimpers, making me chuckle behind her.

Slamming back inside, I dig my fingers into her neck while she squirms beneath me. I can already see bruises blossoming on her skin when I remove my hand to trap her wrists behind her back.

Just then, a car pulls into the lookout. Willow stiffens, trying to push back in order to slink away. Tightening my grip on her, I take her harder, growling in her ear. "Let them watch me fuck you like a slut. You know it turns you on, sweetheart. I can feel you squeeze my dick."

Her response is a loud moan.

The car door opens, and a man steps out. This is why I took her to this lookout. The likelihood of anyone coming here from Skelton is slim. This man is an outsider.

"That's a fine piece of pussy you have there."

"What do you say, sweetheart? Shall we let him watch?"

"Mmm," she whimpers, rocking fast and hard on the hood while I continue fucking her in front of the stranger, feeling a strange sense of power.

Leaning back against the side of his car, he begins to unbuckle his belt, seeing what I'll do. He's a brave fucker.

"Should I let him fuck you? Would you want that?"

I never would. I'm too possessive to share, but I want her to believe that I might lend her to this man. She thrives on danger. I can feel it when her pussy squeezes me.

"Do you think he could fuck you as good as me?"

She tries to shake her head while he shoves his jeans down and begins to stroke his dick. He's not approaching us, which means he knows the deal. He can watch, but he's not allowed to touch what's mine.

"Do you see that?" I whisper in her ear, releasing her

wrists. "He wishes he could swap places with me. You arouse him, Willow."

"Oh god, oh god, oh god," she chants, breasts bobbing as she pushes herself up on her forearms. I like him watching them bob in time with my thrusts.

The man's hand moves quickly and expertly over his cock. Up and down, faster and harder.

I flip her over onto her back and spread her out on the hood. I'm not satisfied until I'm fucking her so hard that her tits bounce wildly, and the wet sounds her pussy makes mix with my grunts and the stranger's panting breaths.

"Holy fuck!" he groans, planting his feet wider.

Grabbing Willow in a choke hold, I tilt my head toward the stranger. The tendons in his neck strain. Once my girl has climaxed, he better get back in his car fast before I kill him for seeing her like this. I both love it and hate it.

Jets of white, stringy cum squirt from his dick in an arc, landing amongst the pinecones on the ground. The sight pushes Willow over the edge, and she comes with a loud scream. Her pussy clamps down on my cock, and it's all I can do not to snap her neck with my hard grip as I release inside her.

When my soul finally returns to my body, I don't pull out, unable to explain this possessive emotion. I don't want my cum to leave her cunt.

"Thanks for that. I pulled in to stretch my legs and got more than I bargained for." The man tightens his belt, then winks at Willow before getting back in his car and driving away.

I reluctantly pull my dick out. Scooping my cum up when it seeps from her cunt, I push it back inside her while she attempts to catch her breath.

Her giggles soon fill the air. "I can't believe that happened."

I tweak her nipple and smirk. "Did you like it?"

She tries to close her legs, but I spread them wide open again, enjoying the sight of her swollen pussy and my cum trickling between her ass cheeks.

Leaning over her, I rip my mask off and drag my tongue through her folds. I circle her too-sensitive clit until she's coming for me a second time. Then I flip her over on her front and squeeze her ass hard. "I want a third."

By the time I'm done with her, the sun has set behind the trees.

CHAPTER 15
WILLOW
FEBRUARY 27TH, 2016

"I'M STARTING to worry about Mom," Liam says a few days later, turning a page in the newspaper while I take a bite of my sandwich. I've snuck out to see Grayson every night. My brother is none the wiser, too busy on his laptop or watching sports on the TV. I keep wondering why he's here and how long he's planning to stay. He was gone for a year and a half, but now he's back?

I roll my eyes.

"Liam," I reply when I've finished chewing, "this is what she's like. She's never home. There's always a lame note, always some excuse."

He looks at me over the paper, like an old grandad. "It's not fair to you, Willow. You're only seventeen."

"I'm two weeks away from turning eighteen."

Shaking his head, he says, "She was always useless but never this bad."

"That's because she worshipped the ground you walked on. Then you left, and I couldn't do anything right."

I'm about to take a second bite out of my sandwich when I pause. Snatching the paper out of his hand, my eyes widen as my eyes scan over the article.

'Luca Shaw, 18, from Skelton, was reported missing by his concerned parents after he failed to return home from school.'

"What the hell?" I whisper, my hands trembling.

"Oi, I was reading that!" Liam shouts after me when I run from the kitchen. After pulling on my Chucks, I exit the house and hurry across the lawn to Grayson's house. Banging my fist on the door, I wrap my arms around myself. It's freezing out here, and I'm only in my sleep shorts and tank top.

As soon as Grayson opens the door, I slam the newspaper against his naked chest. He must have only just woken up. His gray joggers sit low on his hips as he motions for me to enter.

"Did you do something to him?"

"What are you talking about?" Grayson asks.

I follow close on his heels, my heart roaring in my ears.

Pressing his shoulder against the door, he emerges into the kitchen.

I step in after him. "Luca is missing."

"What?" He frowns, and I grab the newspaper. It takes me a few attempts to find the page with the full spread because my hands are trembling too much. I hold it out for him. "Look."

Reading over the article, he looks up at me. "Are you accusing me of this?"

I don't know. Am I? "You said you would hurt him if I fucked him again. Now he's gone."

Tossing the newspaper on the kitchen island, he crosses his arms. "You seriously think I would do something to an eighteen-year-old boy?"

"You threatened to."

"Do you think I murdered my daughter too? That Dylan is innocent?"

"No," I reply, even though my head is a confused mess right now.

With a scoff, he drops his arms. "I can't fucking believe this."

He walks away and I chase after him, pulling him to a stop at the threshold of the hallway. "I didn't mean it that way. Luca is gone... I-I..."

"You what? You thought you would come here and accuse me of murder?"

Needing to feel him close, I wrap my arms around his neck and try to place a kiss on his stubbly cheek, but he easily shoves me off.

"Do you think I killed my wife too? That all these disappearances are because of me?!"

"No," I reply, but my voice is weak and I'm exhausted. Dylan's trial is getting closer. Emotions are running high.

I try to hug him again, but he won't have any of it. Shrugging me off, he walks away, disappearing down the hallway. "Go home, Willow."

"Grayson!" I call out.

Striding back down the hallway, he jabs his finger into my chest. "If you think for one damn second that I killed my wife, daughter, and some fucking eighteen-year-old kid, then you can fuck right off! I've been through hell this year! I don't need your paranoid shit on top of it. Don't you think the cops investigated me, snooping around my home for clues and invading my privacy at a time when I had lost what meant the most to me in the world? My wife. My daughter." His voice breaks and he steps back, shoulders slumping. "Leave, Willow. You're just a kid for crying out loud. What are you doing with a middle-aged man like me? Fucking your dead best friend's father?"

I draw in a sharp, shaky breath as my eyes fill with stinging tears. "You want me gone, Grayson? Is that it? You think I'm naïve because I'm young? That I can't be as fucking holy as your dead wife?"

He slaps me.

Breathing hard, we glare at each other. Grayson, with his hand still raised, and me, cradling my stinging cheek.

Without another word, I walk out.

❄

"I'M GOING BACK HOME," my brother says the next evening, appearing in the doorway to the living room as I'm channel hopping.

"Okay."

Pushing off the doorframe, he steps deeper into the room. I'm wrapped up in my bathrobe on the couch, and he's freshly showered, dressed in jeans and a navy shirt. Looking over my shoulder, I furrow my brows. "Now?"

"No." He takes a seat in the armchair. "I'll stay until after your birthday."

"Oh."

"I, uh, I feel bad leaving you."

I settle on an episode of The Office. "I'm used to it, Liam. Everyone leaves." I meet his eyes, and we stare at each other across the coffee table. The flickering glow from the fireplace casts his face in shadows.

"Will you be okay?"

"I'll be fine."

He nods before flicking his blonde hair out of his eyes. "Will you, uh," he drags his gaze across the room, "ask Mom to phone me when she gets home?"

"Of course." We both know she won't be home for a while. She never is.

Slapping the armrests, he rises to his feet. "I'm going out to meet up with a couple of old friends from high school."

My attention is already back on the TV. "Have fun."

"Don't stay up too late," he says, but the joke falls flat. "I'll see you tomorrow."

I hum in agreement, switching the channel again.

The front door sounds shortly after. The silence that follows drowns out the TV. It doesn't matter how much I turn the volume up. It screams, clawing at my skin until I break down in a sob.

Everyone leaves.

"Willow?"

I release a startled scream and turn in my chair.

Grayson is approaching me warily as if he's unsure if he's welcome or not.

"I saw your brother get in a taxi."

Standing up, I pull my bathrobe closed and tuck my hair behind my ear. "What are you doing here, Grayson?"

"I wanted to talk to you." He holds his hand up as if he means me no harm. "I want to apologize for slapping you." Swallowing hard, he comes to a stop an arm's length away. "I shouldn't have done that."

I stay silent.

"We said some things in the heat of the moment that neither of us meant. You're not a naive young girl. You're funny and smart. You made me smile for the first time since…" He steps even closer until his smell surrounds me, woodsy and warm. "I get it. If I were you, I would march my ass over to my house and ask the same questions you did yesterday."

I shake my head. "No, Grayson. I was wrong. I shouldn't have asked you those questions."

Surging forward, he cups my face. "In between all the crazy fucking, I've truly come to like you, Willow."

"I got scared," I whisper. "When I saw the article about Luca's disappearance, I didn't know what to thi—"

He shuts me up with a kiss, then whispers, "2.8 million kids run away every year."

I smile despite myself. "Did you Google that?"

"After Chloe…"

I cringe. Of course, he googled every possibility after his

daughter's disappearance. I draw in a breath. "After Dylan's arrest, Luca was troubled."

"He'll show up soon," Grayson reassures me, dragging his nose down my cheek and jaw before pulling me closer, placing kisses along the column of my neck.

I melt into him, fisting his T-shirt. His scratchy stubble feels amazing against my skin as he braids his fingers in my hair.

"Please tell me I can fuck you now. I need to be inside you."

"I'm yours, Grayson."

His strong hands grip my hips and lift me up. He guides my legs around his waist, and my arms wrap around his neck as he carries me upstairs to my bedroom.

CHAPTER 16
WILLOW
MARCH 12TH, 2016

MY EYES SCAN over the note on the kitchen island.

Don't forget about the dentist appointment this afternoon.
Mom.

A tap on the window makes me nearly jump out of my skin. It's Grayson.

I place the note back down, then hurry outside into the fresh spring morning. The snow is gone, and the daffodils have made an appearance. "My brother is asleep," I whisper, closing the front door behind me.

Grayson's smile is sinful. He goes to place his arms on either side of me on the door, but I slide out at the last minute. "The neighbors will see."

"You forget one thing, sweetheart," he teases, following behind me when I cross the lawn to his house. I know what he's about to say, but it still makes me smile.

"You're eighteen today. You're legal. I can fuck you all I want."

We've barely made it through the door to his house when he presses me against it and kisses me breathless.

"Is this why you brought me here, Mr. Reid? To have your wicked way with me?"

His lips trail a hot path down my neck. "You think I would pass up on an opportunity like this?"

Giggles climb up my throat when he nuzzles the hollow at my collarbone. "I have to get back before my brother wakes up. He leaves today, and I want to say goodbye."

"I have a surprise for you."

That makes me smile. "You do?"

"You think I would let my girl turn eighteen without buying her a birthday present?"

"Say it again." I bite my lip, arching my neck for him.

"My girl?" His lips return to mine, hot and hungry.

"Does that mean you're my man?"

"Hell yes," he growls, palming my ass and lifting me up.

"Are you going to fuck me in front of a stranger again?"

"You liked that, huh?" He carries me into the kitchen, laying me down on the island in full view of the large window. The cool surface bites into my skin as he sears my inner thighs with his hot breath. His lips trail kisses over my sensitive skin, closer and closer to where I need him the most.

"The blinds…" I trail off, moaning when he presses down on my clit with his thumb.

"You're eighteen, sweetheart. Let them watch me eat you." His fingers hook in my sleep shorts, and he slides them off.

Grabbing my thighs, he spreads me wide open, blowing on my sensitive pussy.

"What's the surprise?" I ask.

"Be a good girl for me, and I'll let you have it after you've come all over my face."

His stubble scratches the inside of my thigh as he bites down on my skin. I whimper, my hips bucking off the island.

"So eager," he chuckles, his amusement vibrating against

my clit. He licks it, causing me to gasp and pull on his short hair. "Any last words?"

"Stop being such a fucking tease, Mr. Reid," I growl, falling back against the marble surface.

"It's Grayson," he replies with a laugh, then covers me with his hot mouth. God, he's sinful, going to town on my pussy like he can't get enough. My back arches off the island, and my hands drag across the surface to grip the edges.

Slapping my clit, he orders, "Moan my name when you come."

Delicious shivers run down my spine as praises pour freely from my lips. His tongue swirls faster and faster, increasing in intensity until a wave of pleasure floods through my body.

Placing one last kiss on my tingling clit, Grayson straightens up. He steps back and licks me off his lips while he watches me catch my breath on his kitchen island.

As I sit up, he opens one of the kitchen drawers and hands me a brown envelope. Placing his hands on either side of me, he smiles against my lips. "Open it, sweetheart."

"What is it?"

His lips brush up against the corner of my mouth, and he whispers, "Open it."

Unable to hold back a smile, I tear open the envelope and peek inside. My eyes flick up to his. "What's this?"

"Plane tickets," he replies, wetting his lips while watching me closely. "When the trial is over, I'm taking you away."

"Paris," I whisper as emotion clogs my throat. "I've always wanted to go there."

"I know. You used to tell me all the time when you were younger. You and Chloe planned to study there together."

I search his brown eyes, unable to stop myself from reaching out to trace my fingertips over his stubbly cheek. His beard rasps beneath my touch. He leans in, sucking my bottom lip between his teeth. "Two weeks. You and me in

Paris. We'll leave all the drama behind. Forget about the trial and the death sentence."

My fingers slide through the soft hair at the nape of his neck. I pull him closer, pressing my lips to his. His kiss is as fervent as mine, and his big hands grab me a little too hard.

"Fuck me, Grayson."

His smile turns wolfish. "Since you asked so nicely."

※

I'M ROOTING through the kitchen drawer—that one we all have where all the shit accumulates—when I hear a grunt followed by several thuds and a loud bang in the hallway. Leaving the drawer open, I run out.

Liam curses at the top of the stairs. "I fucking dropped it."

The floor is covered in a sea of clothes, and his suitcase lies open next to the wall.

Pressing my lips together, I try not to laugh. "Unlucky."

His feet stomp down the stairs while I start collecting his clothes.

"Just shove them in, don't worry about folding them."

Crouched on the floor, we work in silence. When the suitcase is packed, my brother reaches out to take my hand, squeezing gently. "Are you sure you'll be okay?"

"If you feel the need to keep asking, why don't you stay?"

Staring at our clasped hands, he seems to weigh his words. "This isn't my home anymore, sis."

"You mean *I'm* not your home anymore." Tearing my hand away, I rise to my feet. I take a deep breath, feeling exhausted all of a sudden. "I have something for you."

He follows me into the kitchen, where I continue rooting through the drawer while Liam stares at the note on the kitchen table. "What time is your dentist appointment?"

"It's at four," I reply, removing the single key.

"What's this?" Liam asks when I hold it out.

"It's for my Toyota in the garage." I shrug. "I figure you need it more than me."

"I can't accept this."

"Why not?"

He stares at the key in his hand. "It's too generous, for one."

Gripping the counter behind me, my eyes slide over to the window. It's raining outside, lashing against the glass.

"Here, take it." He tries to hand it back.

"You should have it. I don't drive, Liam. I'm not like you. Skelton is my home. I might dream about moving away, but we both know I'll still be here decades from now."

A muscle ticks in his jaw. I know my brother well enough to see the war he's battling. He wants to accept it because we both know he needs a car, but he doesn't like to feel indebted to anyone.

"Take it," I insist. "It's only a rusty little Toyota, but it runs."

"Thanks." He smiles, pulling me in for a hug. "I'll be back again soon, I promise."

We both know it's a lie. But I hug him back and pretend this is my life—that I'm the girl with the caring older brother.

EPILOGUE
OCTOBER 27TH, 2015

CHLOE

"YOU'RE SUCH A FUCKING DICK, DYLAN!"

"Baby," he pleads, pulling me back when I try to walk away. We've been arguing for what feels like hours. I'm cold and tired. "Don't do this. Not over some stupid pictures." Caging me against the side of the house, he presses his forehead to mine. "I love you, Chloe. It was a fucking mistake."

"Love me?" I whisper, my heart splintering in my chest. Dylan has been my world since we were fourteen when he kissed me at Sam's party. "Did you love me when you touched yourself to pictures of her naked body? Did you think of me then? Or did you think of her when you fucked me?"

Stepping back, he spins in a circle and throws his arms out. "For fuck's sake, Chloe! I've told you already; they were just pictures. I don't care about her. She's no one!"

"So you keep saying." With a sigh, I walk past him. "I'm leaving."

I need space away from him to process these feelings

inside me. I'm hurt, angry, and frustrated; even surprised. I truly thought what we had was real.

His fingers wrap around my arm and he pulls me back. "You're not going anywhere."

"Let me go!" I shove him off, but he grabs me around my waist and lifts me up. I kick and scream to no avail; the party is too loud. "Put me down!"

"Jeez, calm yourself," Dylan growls, trapping me against the house. "What can I do right now to make this right? Tell me, baby, and I'll do it. I'll do anything!" Pointing to the side of the house, he continues, "Do you want me to go tell her to stop sending me nudes? Is that it? Want me to tell her she's got nothing on you? Because I will if that's what it'll take. I'll let everyone at this fucking party know you're the only one for me. I made a mistake, Chloe—a damn mistake!"

"I want you to let me go," I hiss. I'm tired and angry. I just want him to leave me alone.

"The fuck I will!" he growls, trapping my wrists.

We struggle some more until one of Dylan's drunk friends, Logan, comes stumbling around the corner. "Hey, dude, the guys are wondering where you are."

With his hands on his hips, Dylan stares at me for a long moment before sighing defeatedly. "I'll be back in a bit, okay? I'm talking to my girl right now."

Logan sways on the spot, then lets out a chortle. "I see what this is. I interrupted something, didn't I? You were about to fuck. Don't mind me. I'm leaving."

With a wink and a salute, he disappears around the corner.

I shoulder past Dylan, and he lets out an angry roar. "Dammit, Chloe! Why are you so fucking stubborn?!"

Half turning, I spit, "Why don't you go find her, Dylan? I'm sure she'll let you fuck her tonight."

Shaking his head, he releases a bitter chuckle before

scratching his chin. "Fine, whatever. I'm done!" Without another word, he storms off.

My heart thunders in my chest as I watch him turn the corner.

Fucking asshole.

The walk home is long and cold. I should have caught a lift with Willow and Luca or asked Jenny to drive me. If my father knew I was walking home alone this late, he would ground me for the next year. He's always on my case.

"Make sure you get a lift home. Don't walk alone."

About halfway, I start to cry. I don't want to be upset. I want to be angry. I want to hate Dylan for the photographs I found on his phone. Pictures of her, naked on her flowery bedspread, surrounded by fluffy white throw pillows. I can still picture her dark hair spread around her like a halo while she photographed herself tweaking her nipples. How could Dylan do this to me? Did he imagine himself fucking her when he jerked off to those pictures? Of course, he did. Why else would he message her, asking for more?

I don't want to be alone with my thoughts, not tonight.

My feet carry me up Willow's driveway. The house is dark except for a faint flickering light in the window beside the front door. The TV in the living room is on. She's up late, binge-watching Bloodline or Dark Matter. She won't stop talking about either.

I ring the doorbell because I know her mom is out, so I don't need to worry about waking anyone.

The light in the hallway flicks on, and the door opens, revealing Willow in her pink robe.

"I didn't wake you, did I?"

I know I look a mess with mascara streaks and strands of hair drying to my cheeks.

She steps aside so I can enter. No sooner has the door shut than she squeezes me to her. "Are you okay?"

More tears fall. "Breakups suck!"

Leaning back, she searches my eyes. "You broke up?"

"He had naked pictures of her on his phone." I leave the words hanging in the air. Nothing else is said as she leads me into the living room, where I curl up on her couch and wrap myself in a blanket.

Willow disappears into the kitchen and returns with two glasses. She hands me one and sits down on the armchair.

"What's this?" I ask, sniffing the drink. It's definitely alcohol.

"I raided my mom's liquor cabinet. It's gin."

I take a sip. It's dry with a noticeable pine flavor. I'm not sure if I like it or not, but I'll drink anything if it numbs this insistent ache in my chest.

"Do you want to talk about it?" Willow asks.

I take another big sip, letting the cool liquid slip down my throat. "I told him to fuck her."

Willow winces, and for some odd reason, it makes me laugh. I don't know how to feel. My head is such a messed-up place. I thought I had all the chess pieces where I wanted them, only for a busty cheerleader to sweep her arm over my board and scatter them all.

"Will you take him back if he apologizes?"

"He's already apologized a hundred times tonight. It seems to be the only thing he has to say." I imitate him, "'I didn't mean it, Chloe. It was a mistake. I'm sorry.'"

Willow laughs softly when I mutter, "Dipshit!"

I finish my drink, then place it down on the table. "I plan on becoming a hermit after this. No more boys. Ever. I don't care how charming they are with their dimples and broad shoulders."

"You say that now," Willow teases.

I smile, touching my fingers to my cheeks. My face feels strangely weird, almost numb.

"Does Dylan know you're here?"

My sluggish head shakes.

"Good," she replies.

When I lift my head off the couch, the room blurs, the walls distorting. "What's happening?"

"Hmm?" Willow looks away from the TV.

I try to sit up, but my body is too heavy. "I feel weird."

"Oh that," she says, getting to her feet. I'm vaguely aware of her crouching in front of me and slapping my cheek. "I gave you a little something, is all."

My brows pull down low, and when I try to speak, my tongue won't obey. Willow lifts my arm and drops it. It falls on the armrest like a dead weight.

"What's happening?" I slur, struggling to move my head.

"Have I ever told you," she murmurs, stroking her fingers down my cheek, "how tired I am of being the perfect daughter? The perfect sister? The perfect *best friend?* It's exhausting to pretend I'm this version of myself you all want me to be."

She leans closer, cupping my chin and sweeping her eyes over my face. "That's why I killed her, you know?"

My heart thuds heavily in my chest as she climbs to her feet. Metal glints in her hand, and she holds it up when she sees my distress. "It's a knife, Chloe. Don't worry, I won't use it to kill you. I just need to collect some of your blood." She exits the room. Panic presses on my sternum, fighting desperately for a way out as I try to process what's happening. My head is a fog.

Dozens of creased notes rain over me in a cloud of confetti. She slaps my cheek again. "Hey, bestie, don't go to sleep on me yet. See this?" She holds up a note. "Mom wrote me lots of these."

She proceeds to read out a few. "'I'll be gone for the weekend. Help yourself to food in the fridge.' 'I left early. Your dinner money is in the envelope.'"

"Hey, hey, hey." She slaps me again. Once… twice… "Eyes on me."

"Notes," I slur because it's all I can get out as the room starts to spin.

"I kept them throughout the years." She sets fire to one with a lighter, watching the small flame grow in size. "Hundreds of them. After I killed her, well, every morning, I would reach for one in the shoebox beneath my bed and leave it in the kitchen somewhere. It's like she's still here. Sometimes, I swear I can see her in the house." The laughter that climbs up her throat has a crazed quality to it. "It's not like much has changed. Instead of her writing the notes, I pick them out."

"Wh-wh-why?"

"Why what?" she asks, extinguishing the flame and stroking my hair away from my shoulder. "Why did I kill my mom?" Pressing down on my pulse point, she smiles when she feels it racing beneath her fingertips. "I'd had enough of her rejection. See, that's the thing. Your father loves you. You're his entire world. He would walk through fire for you. I'm alone, Chloe. No one gives a shit about me. Not even you, not since we were eleven and Dylan, with his stupid skateboard tricks, smiled at you from the sidewalk. Ever since then, I've been your shadow."

A tear seeps out of the corner of my eye. Swiping it away with her thumb, she soothes me. "It's okay, bestie. It won't hurt. You'll go to sleep, that's all. Won't it be nice to finally join your mom?"

A whimper escapes my lips, and Willow leans in to press her mouth against mine as if she wants to taste the pitiful sound.

"I killed your mom in the same way. I gave her a little something when she came over to help me with my homework. She was my first kill. I'd grabbed my mom's sleeping pills from the bathroom cabinet. It was quick. Mrs. Reid drank her tea and fell asleep. Right here where you are now. It's easy to smother someone when they're unconscious. You just place a pillow over their head and wait."

Sliding down the strap of my dress, she palms my breast, soothing me when more whimpers dance between our lips. "You should blame your father for this, Chloe. It's his fault. I wouldn't have to hurt people if he didn't make me feel this way."

"Please," I choke out, my eyes rolling in their sockets.

"Bestie, hey, don't go to sleep!" She slaps me harder this time. "You have no fucking idea how good your life is. How lucky you are to have a man like Mr. Reid to dote on you. You're his princess, the apple of his eye." Gripping my chin, she snarls, "*I* want to be the apple of his eye. I want him to look at me the way he looked at your mom. I want him to see only me."

Choked sobs escape my lips. Pitiful whimpers of fear. Pleading sounds that'll never form into words.

"It's okay," she whispers, kissing my cheek. "You can go to sleep now. That's it, good girl. Close your eyes."

A soft kiss on my parted lips. "I'll look after Daddy now."

The end.

ALSO BY HARLEIGH BECK

Counter Bet:
Counter Bet
Devil's Bargain

The Rivals:
The Rivals' Touch
Fadeaway

Standalones:
Kitty Hamilton
Sweet Taste of Betrayal

ACKNOWLEDGMENTS

Thank you for reading my novella. I hope you enjoyed the crazy ride. Let me know if you figured out the part where I first revealed the killer.

As always, there are a few people I would like to thank.

Paula — my ride-and-die psycho friend. I love you, and I would slaughter a fucking dragon to keep you safe against the demons in my head.

My hubby — For reading my books when I toss them at him and say, "Proofread this." The poor, long-suffering man never bats an eyelid.

Chris, my editor — Where would I be without you? I no longer cringe when you edit the sex scenes. Can you believe it? It's a miracle.

Heidi — Because you're amazing. Move to England so we can go to a Metallica concert together.

Hannah, my proofreader — You never disappoint. Thank you for proofreading yet another book of mine.

Ndune — You're the sweetest. You're always supportive and have a heart of gold.

Katherine — You message me every single day to say hi, and it means the world.

3Crows Author Services — I'm in love with the cover!

ABOUT THE AUTHOR

Harleigh Beck lives in a small town in the northeast of England. When she's not writing, you'll find her head down in a book. She mainly reads dark romance, but she also likes the occasional horror. She has more books planned, so be sure to connect with on her social media for updates.

Printed in Dunstable, United Kingdom